Joey suddenly caught everyone's attention. "I've got a great idea. Let's find out who's better. Girls or boys. Cindy or Grant."

"How?" Duffy asked as Grant leaned forward.

"A contest. A surfing contest," Joey explained. "We could hold it at the Big Luau next week."

"Well," Grant mumbled, looking from face to face at the excited kids all around him. For a second Cindy thought he was going to decline— which was exactly what she wanted to do.

But then Joey piped up again. "Afraid Cindy will win?"

Nicole shot a withering glance at Joey and, turning to Cindy, said quickly under her breath, "Don't do it."

But before Cindy could think, she heard Grant saying, "Of course not. It's a great idea. We can settle this thing once and for all. That is, if Cindy's not afraid of losing."

And then Cindy heard herself saying, "You bet."

FAWCETT GIRLS ONLY BOOKS

Sisters

THREE'S A CROWD #1

TOO LATE FOR LOVE #2

THE KISS #3

SISTERS

TOO LATE
FOR LOVE

Jennifer Cole

FAWCETT GIRLS ONLY • NEW YORK

RLI: $\dfrac{\text{VL: Grades 5 \& up}}{\text{IL: Grades 6 \& up}}$

A Fawcett Girls Only Book
Published by Ballantine Books
Copyright © 1986 by Cloverdale Press, Inc.

Library of Congress Catalog Card Number: 86-91087

ISBN 0-449-13005-3

Manufactured in the United States of America

First Edition: May 1986
Fifth Printing: October 1988

Chapter 1

*F*riday afternoon, Cindy Lewis walked out of seventh-period biology lab thinking about sophomore year and sand dollars.

As she elbowed her way through the crowded hallway of Vista High, she felt pretty convinced that sophomore year was destined to be one of the most peculiar years of her life. It had started when school began and her parents had flown off on a trip to Japan—leaving the three Lewis sisters at home for an adventure-filled two weeks on their own. While they had been gone, Cindy had suffered a mild concussion in a sailboat accident. Now they were back, and she'd managed to break her own record for detentions: twice in one week. Once for dumping soapsuds in the pool of a rival school just before a swim meet, and once for something so silly she didn't even want to think about it.

Not that being fifteen and in her second year of high school was all that bad. Even the disasters of the last couple of weeks had been kind of fun. But these days everything seemed slightly out of sync. Somehow over the summer everyone and everything in Cindy's world had changed. And Cindy wasn't sure she had changed with it. She felt as if she were squeezed into a pair of comfortable old sneakers that no longer fit.

Just that morning over breakfast, Nicole had diagnosed Cindy's troubles as an acute case of the sophomore slump. "It happens to everyone!" Nicole had declared in that faintly superior older-sister way of hers, looking distastefully at Cindy's beloved, slightly torn Dodgers' T-shirt. Cindy had glared back at Nicole's lacy blouse and her black coffee and neatly sliced half-grapefruit, and defiantly poured herself a third bowl of Wheaties.

Cindy was too aware that Nicole disapproved of the way Cindy dressed, and that fact annoyed Cindy. But not half as much as the fact that Nicole seemed to be right on target about sophomore slump; although Cindy wasn't sure if "slump" was the right word for how she felt.

At least Nicole's dire predictions about biology had been wrong. She had been nuts to listen to her sister. Nicole thought worms and snakes were slimy, and she screamed every time seaweed caught on her legs down at the beach. Besides, Nicole hadn't had Miss Harris for biology.

This afternoon Miss Harris had dissected a live sand dollar for the class. Cindy's stomach hadn't even gone queasy. In fact, today's lab period had convinced her that she'd grow up to be a marine biologist just like Miss Harris. Her favorite teacher had just come back from a field research stint in Baja and was full of nifty information about tube worms and other exotic marine life that flourished off the California coast. She had even promised to organize a field trip to Baja before Christmas for anyone who was interested. Tonight Cindy would ask her dad if she could sign up on Monday. After all, none of her detentions had been for anything *really* serious.

"Hey, Lewis! Wake up!" A familiar voice broke into Cindy's thoughts. Cindy whirled around. At first she couldn't see Duffy Duncan's red head in the crowd. All one thousand Vista High students seemed to be making a beeline for the exit doors at once. Then there was a resounding whack on her back that almost sent her flying.

"Ouch! Duffy, would you cut that out!" Cindy complained, vaguely disoriented by having to look up at his friendly freckled face. She still hadn't quite gotten used to Duffy towering over her. Just this past June, she and her oldest surfing buddy had been exactly the same height: five foot six inches. But Duffy had somehow managed to return from summer at his uncle's Wyoming dude ranch, three inches taller. In fact, suddenly every guy she'd been hanging out with since junior high was taller than she was. Cindy wasn't sure what she thought about that either. She only knew that having to crane her neck to talk to Duffy was yet another in a line of recent changes she wasn't quite sure she liked.

"Am I glad to see you!" Duffy slung one arm over Cindy's shoulder as they proceeded toward her locker. A few feet down the hall, he stopped suddenly and stared intently at Cindy's shirt. "You're going to the Dodgers' game tonight, aren't you?" His tone was half-accusing.

Cindy grinned. "At least someone around here looks excited and a little jealous of that fact! My dad got box seats for the game of the year, and if they win and go on to the playoffs against the Mets and the World Series, he's promised to get tickets for that. Not that Anna cared when I told her at lunch!" Cindy snorted, but bit her lip to keep herself from saying more. Her best friend, Anna, had suddenly gotten her first real crush on—of all people—Duffy Duncan. Now Cindy couldn't very well complain about her to him.

"She's nuts. I'm jealous. But it's too bad you're going," Duffy said sadly.

"Why?" asked Cindy.

"I thought we could head down to the beach and catch a few waves. I want you to meet this great new surfer. His name's Grant MacPhearson, and he's from Hawaii. It's his first day at Vista, and I discovered him gaping at the surfing trophies outside Coach Roscoe's office. Apparently there's a rumor in the Islands that California has no waves worth mentioning."

Cindy's eyebrows shot up, but before she could defend her beloved Santa Barbara beaches, Duffy was waving energetically toward her locker. A tall, dark-haired guy Cindy had never seen before was standing there, his back toward them.

"There he is. I told him to meet us by your locker. Hey, Grant!" Duffy bellowed.

Grant turned around as Cindy and Duffy approached. "Duffy!" He smiled a broad happy smile that looked slightly lopsided, and his right cheek had a deep dimple. As he turned from Duffy to Cindy, Cindy found herself staring up into a pair of piercing blue-green eyes. They matched her own perfectly; though, since he was wearing a turquoise sweat shirt, they looked more green than blue. And today Cindy's eyes more or less looked Dodger blue, like the lettering on her T-shirt. For a second Cindy was tongue-tied. Then she remembered that this guy was from Hawaii and had a lesson to learn about California surfing.

Her voice held just the hint of a challenge as she said easily, "Hi, Grant! I'm Cindy. Cindy Lewis. Welcome to Santa Barbara." But even as she spoke, she surprised herself by thinking that with his incredibly broad shoulders, white teeth, and perfectly even dark tan, Grant MacPhearson fit her kid sister Mollie's description of a hunk to a T.

"Hi, Cindy," Grant said, looking from Cindy to Duffy, who still had his arm slung casually across the blond girl's shoulder. "I hear you're pretty heavily into surfing. Me too."

Cindy suddenly felt uncomfortable with Duffy's arm around her. She stepped slightly away and shifted her books from one slim hip to the other. As she started fiddling with the combination on her locker, she replied, "I guess I am."

"You *guess* you are?" Duffy scoffed and this time whacked Grant across the shoulder. "Mac-Phearson, she's super. In fact, at least three of those trophies you saw outside the gym were Cindy's. Including the one for the California state-wide women's surfing championship. And she was just fourteen when she won that! Plus a couple of those swimming trophies too. You're talking to the apple of Coach Roscoe's eye."

"I believe that!" Grant said. Cindy looked up quickly and met Grant's eyes. He held her glance for a long instant. When she looked away she felt confused and a little bit flattered. Duffy never looked at her like that.

As Cindy turned back to her locker, Duffy rambled on. "Grant won a couple of trophies too, back in Hawaii."

"Aw, they're nothing," Grant protested modestly. "I mean, the surfers back home are out of sight. I'm just your basic Joe Average in that department."

Something in Grant's voice made Cindy grin.

He didn't look like Joe Average, and she could tell he knew it. With his build, he probably didn't surf like Joe Average either. "I bet you're better than that," Cindy ventured, looking up at him again. Beneath the cut-off sleeves of his sweat shirt, his arms were lean and muscular.

Grant flashed a mischievous smile. He leaned against an adjacent locker, watching her flub her combination three times. Finally the door sprang open, revealing the torn poster of a windsurfer who looked remarkably like Grant, except with ordinary blue eyes. Cindy hastily stashed her books inside, removed her portable stereo, and slammed the door shut on the jumble of gym clothes and swimming gear. It was positively humiliating, having Grant see that poster. Even though she had never set eyes on him before this afternoon, it looked like a pinup of him.

At that thought Cindy did something she'd never done before—at least over a guy: She blushed. "Drat!" she muttered to herself, grateful that at that moment Duffy was giving Grant a verbal rundown on the ground-floor vending machines. She took a couple of deep breaths, and her cheeks began to feel cooler. What was the matter with her anyway?

Only as they started walking away from her locker did Cindy remember two things: She had forgotten to take home her Spanish homework, and she was supposed to meet Nicole and Mollie any minute now, in front of her locker. She kept walking anyway.

"So, are you going to join us down on the beach?" Grant asked. "I'm dying to see the Vista High legend in action."

Cindy was vaguely aware that Grant's words held a double meaning. She stuffed her hands in her pockets and took another deep breath before responding. She could tell another blush was coming on.

"Not today. I'm going to the ball game tonight, with my dad." She raked her fingers through her short blond hair and looked Grant directly in the eye.

"Would you believe it, Grant? She's lucked out and gotten tickets for the biggest game of the year. Leave it to a Lewis!" Duffy complained good-naturedly.

Grant seemed to notice Cindy's shirt for the first time. "Ah, a Dodgers fan. That's great. In fact, I'm more or less a Dodgers fan too."

Cindy gave a puzzled frown. For a second it didn't make sense. Grant wasn't from California.

Grant answered her unspoken question. "Back home, everyone's either a Dodgers, Angels, or Giants fan. Although some people root for the Mets or the Yankees."

"The Yankees!" Cindy gasped. "They're our mortal enemies!"

Grant laughed and threw up his hands in mock surrender, backing away a few steps. "Sorry. Not me, though. I'm rooting for the Dodgers. In fact, I have to admit I'm really jealous. About your going to the game, that is. I've never been to a major league game. That's one of the few disadvantages to Hawaii."

"You haven't?" Cindy and Duffy cried in unison.

Grant shook his head wistfully. "In fact, I'm not even sure who L.A.'s playing tonight."

"Cincinnati! They're tied for first place in the Western Division." Duffy snorted in disbelief.

"Right!" Grant grinned sheepishly. "How could I forget?"

Cindy suddenly felt sorry for Grant. He must be sixteen or seventeen years old, and he'd never been to a baseball game. "If it weren't the last game tonight, maybe my dad could scare up an extra ticket for you," she said, suddenly wishing her father could manage to pull a few strings by tonight. She slouched against the door leading out onto the sunny front lawn of the school. "Too bad I can't go with you guys tonight. But no way. Dad would kill me if I skipped the game."

"*I'd* kill you if you skipped the game!" Duffy roared, then added teasingly, "Unless you give me the ticket."

Cindy glared at him. "No way."

"Okay, then. I want to hear your on-the-spot report, tomorrow morning, first thing, down on the beach," Duffy said.

"Right," Grant echoed. "First thing tomorrow I'll be down there, too." Grant held Cindy's eyes a second, then picked up his backpack and slung it over his shoulder.

As Duffy pushed open the double glass doors, he turned back. "See you then, Cindy, and be ready to show Grant your stuff."

"You'll be there?" Grant asked, not taking his eyes off of Cindy's smiling face.

Cindy's smile widened. "You bet! The honor of Santa Barbara is at stake. See you then," she called back over her shoulder as she quickly jogged toward her locker and right into Mollie.

"*Who* was that?" Mollie's petite body sank in a mock faint against the wall as she rolled her big blue eyes up toward the ceiling. "He's a real hunk!"

Cindy groaned. "Mollie Lewis, you have a one-track mind. He's just a new guy, that's all." She shrugged, though she didn't feel quite as casual as she sounded.

"That's all?" Mollie asked while trying to keep pace with her taller sister's long stride. "I mean, in the entire freshman class of new people there's no new guy like that. I mean not half a new guy like that."

Cindy inhaled deeply and pursed her lips. It didn't work. She burst out, "Mollie, just because he's male doesn't make him a sex object. Give me a break, will you?"

A couple of senior guys lounging by the Coke machine winked at Mollie as she scampered by. Tossing her wavy blond hair off her face, she smiled a small self-satisfied smile, pretending to ignore their comments about her snug red sweater. As soon as the two sisters were safely beyond the guys, her eyes narrowed. "Cindy, I bet he's a junior. Maybe even a senior. Where's he from, anyway? How long have you been keeping him from me? I'll kill you if he's been in one of your classes all along and you didn't tell me about him."

Cindy struggled to keep her temper as she approached her locker. Her father had given her a long lecture a few months back about how inappropriate it was for a fifteen-going-on-sixteen-year-old girl to punch her fourteen-going-on-fifteen-year-old sister. But that was before Mollie had entered high school. Since then she had been twice as impossible to live with. As Cindy violently whirled the dial on her combination lock, she tried to ignore Mollie's babble.

Nicole's soft clear voice rang out across the nearby empty hall. "Sorry I'm late. The Student Council meeting went on and on." Her gray-blue eyes narrowed as she looked into Cindy's locker. "Oh, what a mess."

"Not as bad as mine," Mollie said. "Hey, that guy looks just like *him*." She tapped her finger against the windsurfer poster.

"I know, I know," Cindy moaned, yanking out her Spanish book and quickly slamming the locker shut.

While Nicole adjusted the combs in her silky

shoulder-length brown hair she smiled indulgently at Mollie. "I suppose I should ask, Like whom? And what are *you* so upset about?" she added to Cindy, who turned her back on Nicole as an answer.

"The hottest hunk to hit town in ages. He was just hanging out with Duffy and Cindy over there by the door. And from the way he was looking at Cindy . . ." Mollie giggled slyly.

"Shut up!" Cindy exclaimed. What was Mollie talking about, anyway? "Nicole, don't encourage her. Please. There's this new guy. Duffy met him today. I don't even know what year he is. He's from Hawaii and he's a surfer and we were talking about surfing together. That's all!" She glared at Mollie.

But Mollie ignored Cindy completely. "I mean, I thought he was asking her out for a date. For tonight," Mollie exclaimed as the three girls headed for the bike racks along the western edge of the parking lot.

"What's his name? Maybe I know him," Nicole said.

Mollie tugged Cindy's sleeve. "Out with it. You've hoarded him long enough."

Cindy shook her head in disgust and mumbled, "Grant. Grant MacPhearson," as the three sisters pedaled onto the road.

By the time the girls pulled into the large circular driveway in front of the Lewises' roomy red Spanish-style house, Cindy didn't ever want to hear Grant MacPhearson's name again. Maybe she'd skip going down to the beach tomorrow. Mollie was so intent on making something of the fact that Grant had looked at her in *that* way, it was sickening.

"Hi, Winston!" Mollie dumped her bike on the lawn and bounded halfway across the grass to throw her arms around the enormous, black Newfoundland dog loping across the yard to greet them.

While Nicole and Cindy put their bikes away, Nicole asked, "Cindy, why don't you go down to the beach tonight? It's a perfect opportunity."

Cindy raised her eyebrows and threw her hands up in the air. "I don't get it. What's the big deal? *All* the guys are down at the beach tonight. It's Friday. Duffy just wanted to celebrate because Grant's new in town. Don't you get the point, Nicole? It's just about surfing. He's not even a friend"—Cindy surprised herself by adding—"yet."

Nicole smoothed her blouse over the top of her trim black pants and shook her head. "I don't get it. Cindy, you're fifteen years old, and you'd rather go to a stupid ball game with Dad than spend an evening with a great-looking guy."

"Ball games are not stupid!" Cindy retorted, then added with a disgusted toss of her head, "Oh, shut up. I'm not in the mood for one of your lectures. Anyway, if he's a surfer, I'll see enough of him to make all of you happy."

Mollie walked up in time to hear Cindy's last

few words. "Great!" she squealed, and clapped her hands. "I knew deep down inside you really liked him. *I* could tell."

"Stop it," Cindy suddenly yelled. "Both of you. Sometimes I think you're from another century. Guys aren't just for boyfriends. Anyway, I don't even know if I like him—as a person." With that, Cindy scooped up their cat, Smokey, and stormed into the house. Even from the lawn her sisters could hear her slam the door to her room. Winston gave a worried whine and trotted up to Nicole to nuzzle her hand.

"What's with her!" Mollie exclaimed, wide-eyed and looking a bit hurt.

Nicole thoughtfully shook her head. "I don't know. Not really. Unless ..." Nicole started into the house, Winston at her heels.

"Unless what?" Mollie asked, entering the kitchen and automatically opening the refrigerator, then abruptly slamming it shut, remembering she was only one day into her three-week banana diet.

"You know what, Mollie?" Nicole said. She bit her lip and giggled and lowered her voice to a whisper. "I think our tomboy sister is on the verge of her first real crush!"

"I knew it!" Mollie yelled, then clapped her hand over her mouth. "I mean, if you could have seen this guy, you would have forgotten about your beloved Mark Russell in an instant. Grant What's-his-name is the cutest thing to come along in ages and ages. Oh, Nicole!" Mollie suddenly looked panic-stricken. "What if she blows it? I mean, Cindy's so convinced she's never going to fall in love and all that stuff."

Nicole sank down on a kitchen chair and reached for an apple. "I know. If only she would listen to me."

Mollie sat down beside Nicole and absently scratched Winston behind the ears. "Maybe she won't *listen,* but I bet we can help her anyway ... without her even knowing."

"Mollie!" Nicole warned. "Stay out of this. I don't think we need one of your harebrained plans at this point."

"What plan?" Mollie asked innocently. She had no plan in mind. At least not yet.

Chapter 2

*M*ollie Lewis held the firm belief that Saturdays didn't officially begin until afternoon—*late* afternoon. Today, however, Mollie had scraped herself out of bed at seven and, after struggling to perfect her makeup through half-closed eyes, had tagged along after Cindy, supposedly to get some exercise in her new red leather sneakers—and her equally new red-and-black polka dot bikini. All during breakfast she had talked about Day Two of her banana diet and Day One of her *Firm New You* aerobic workout program. Of course, Mollie's real motive for getting up early on a Saturday was Day One of the romance between Cindy and Grant MacPhearson, which she insisted was inevitable.

Mollie planted her hands on her tanned hips and said in an exasperated tone of voice, *"Now* where'd she go to?"

She and Nicole were standing on top of the rocks just north of the beach. Only a minute before, Cindy had been walking alongside them. Now she had vanished. Mollie, shading her eyes with her hand, peered back into the morning sun. But the road leading up toward the house was deserted, and Cindy's yellow-and-black suited figure was nowhere to be seen. Mollie shook her head, gave a perplexed sigh, then turned back to study the crowd gathered below them on the sand.

Nicole didn't bother to answer. At that moment she was wondering whatever had possessed her to leave her cozy room and her Jane Austen novel to join her sisters in this crazy morning escapade. Of course, Cindy *always* went surfing early in the morning. Every Saturday since junior high she had gotten up at dawn and jogged some disgusting number of miles up and down the hill in the park near their house. Then she'd gorge herself on a humongous breakfast and race right down to join her surfer friends. All of this took place hours before Nicole had even the faintest desire to budge from the house.

Nicole yawned, delicately covering her mouth with her hand. Then she proceeded to rub her upper arms and imagine a thermos of hot coffee. She didn't care what Mollie or Cindy said, it was

definitely not a warm morning—not in her book.
Cool air, lingering fog, and a crowd of kids gathered on the beach with their surfboards definitely
wasn't Nicole's idea of Saturday fun. The only
consolation was that her boyfriend, Mark, was
probably already down on the beach with his
friends from the track team. He'd be finished running by now, and maybe he'd take her somewhere for a nice warm hot chocolate. She stuffed
her hands into the pockets of her pink beach
jacket, and shivered. *"Il fait froid,"* she murmured,
and smiled. Nicole was crazy about France—for
that matter, she was interested in anything French,
from food to art to fashions—and saying "I'm
cold" in French made her feel better.

Mollie suddenly gasped and pointed beyond a
clump of palm trees over toward the surfing
crowd's favorite patch of beach. "Look, Nicole,
look! That's him! Over there."

Nicole squinted and pushed up the brim of her
straw sunhat. Instantly, she spotted the tall dark-
haired guy in a pair of red, black, and blue print
surfing trunks, standing in the middle of a group
of boys. Even from this distance, Nicole could see
that he was taller and more muscular than most
of the boys. A few yards away, Anna and Carey
and a couple of other girls from Cindy's crowd
lay sprawled on their beach towels. They were
laughing and talking excitedly and kept glancing
over at the guys. Nicole couldn't hear them over
the noise of the surf, but she could tell they were

trying to get the attention of the new guy. And no wonder. Mollie sure was right this time: Grant MacPhearson was certainly worth watching.

Nicole nodded thoughtfully and said, "I bet he's at least a junior. Look at those muscles."

"Muscles!" Mollie repeated in an awed tone of voice, then giggled. "See what I mean, Nicole? Isn't Cindy crazy? Going to a ball game with Dad instead of hanging out with that guy. Where is she, anyway?"

A familiar woof-woof and the pad of doggy paws partially answered Mollie's question. Winston bounded up, sniffed at the sea breeze, and gleefully raced down into the water. Cindy jogged into sight a second later.

"Where have you been?" Mollie grumbled as she started down the path toward the beach.

"Someone left the gate open." Cindy glared at Mollie, then continued. "I saw Winston following us down the road. I didn't want him jumping in any of the neighbors' pools again, so I made sure I got him to come with us." Cindy hoisted her beach bag over her shoulder, and balanced her surfboard under her arm and bounced across the sand. "I wonder who's here," she said.

"Oh, the usual crowd," Nicole replied with a straight face.

"Nicole!" Mollie glared at her sister over her shoulder. Nicole winked at her, and Mollie looked puzzled for a minute and then grinned as she added with a big bored yawn, "In fact who else would be crazy enough to hit the beach at ten A.M. on a Saturday? Nothing happens in this town until four P.M." she concluded, recalling the line from a movie she had seen the night before on late-night TV.

But Cindy didn't seem to be paying any attention. She had spotted her friends gathered on the beach to the right of the parking lot in front of Salty Dog's Snack Shack. "Anna's here! And Carey and everybody!" She whooped and raced ahead of Mollie toward the girls. "They won! They won!" she shouted, and then the pounding surf drowned out the rest of her words.

Mollie stood openmouthed. "How can she think of baseball at a time like this!"

"Easy. Cindy doesn't know she has a crush yet." Nicole laughed. "Besides, your hunk has pulled a disappearing act." Sure enough, Grant was suddenly nowhere to be seen.

Mollie snorted her disapproval and scanned the groups of kids, looking for Grant. "Well, if she doesn't watch out, some other girl's going to get him first. And if she really isn't interested, I know someone who *is.*"

"Mollie Lewis," Nicole scolded. "Hands off. You yourself said he seemed to like Cindy. Anyway, he's definitely too old for you—like Brett!"

Mollie shrugged sheepishly. "I'm not going to *steal* him from Cindy. It's just that if she doesn't care about him— And as for Brett," Mollie declared defensively, "I handled him just fine." She was referring to a senior guy she had hung out with at the Lewis sisters' now infamous party the weekend before.

"Winston handled him just fine," Nicole reminded her briskly. "Look, there's Mark. You go find your own friends. Isn't that Sarah and Linda over there?" Nicole pointed toward a cluster of freshmen, one of whom was waving energetically toward Mollie. Mollie waved back and, wearing a martyred expression on her face, reluctantly trotted off to join the girls sitting a discreet distance from about a dozen freshman guys playing volleyball.

"So how come your sisters are here so early?" Anna gestured toward Nicole and Mollie as they walked their separate ways down the beach.

Cindy turned around just in time to see Mark run toward Nicole and hug her. Cindy shrugged and absently petted a very wet Winston. "Beats me. Seems to be the latest fad in the Lewis household. Getting up early on Saturday. Mollie probably read in *Seventeen* that early to rise was good for your complexion." Cindy stabbed at the sand with her finger, then looked hard at Anna. "You know, you could be a bit more excited—I mean, the Dodgers won—they'll probably beat the Mets—and all you care about is my sisters. What's with you, anyway?"

"What's with *me*?" Anna grumbled, flipping her long brown hair and rummaging in her bag for some lip gloss. "You're the one that's been out of it ever since school began." She held up a mirror and carefully studied a small red blotch on her chin. "Oh, darn, a zit!"

"Oh, keep quiet," Cindy said sharply, and began smearing a layer of white sunblock on her nose. Even though it was early, she could feel her nose burning again. Freckles were bad enough, but a peeling red nose was definitely something Cindy hated. Just then she noticed that Anna was wearing a new bathing suit—a bronze bikini that almost matched her tan and played up her long, curvy figure.

"That suit's new," Cindy commented. She had to admit Anna looked good in a bikini, but tank suits were so much more practical for surfing.

Anna smiled. "Do you like it?" She lowered her voice. "Do you think Duffy will like it?"

Carey broke in. "If not, he's crazy, and not worth it. If he doesn't call you now and ask you to that homecoming dance, I think you should look elsewhere. After all, there are other fish in the sea," she added, giving a significant little nod back over her shoulder.

Cindy sighed. Here they go again, she thought. All Anna and Carey ever talked about nowadays was guys. No, that wasn't quite fair, she reminded herself. Sometimes, they still talked about baseball and swimming. After all, Anna was the fiercest competitor on the girls' baseball team and would probably be captain next year, and Carey was the best high-diver on the Vista High girls' squad. But off the field and out of the water, all they talked about was boys and dances and dates, and it was beginning to make Cindy sick.

"Cindy, you're not listening." Carey shook her by the shoulder. "There's this new guy. Anna may be too lovesick over Duncan to really notice, but he's unbelievable. And you should see him surf." Carey's dark brown eyes sparkled with excitement.

"A surfer?" Cindy said, then flopped down and began doing some quick situps. She did seven before she added casually, "You mean Grant MacPhearson. I wonder how good he really is," Cindy said in a cool, smooth voice. Actually she didn't feel so cool and easy about this Grant MacPhearson. In fact, at the moment she felt disappointed. The first thing that she had noticed when she got to the beach was that Grant was nowhere in sight. The second thing was that the surf was very rough.

"How do you know him? You were at the game last night," Carey gasped, a note of jealousy creeping into her voice.

Cindy couldn't help smiling a little. "Oh, I met him yesterday afternoon. He told me he'd be down here this morning. He doesn't believe Californians are really good surfers—probably chickened out. The waves probably scared him last night."

"Scared him?" Carey scoffed. "Well, they aren't scaring him now. Look out there."

Anna commented breathlessly, "He's the only person who's gone out today."

As Cindy followed Carey's glance over the water, her first thought was, What had happened to Anna's single-minded devotion to Duffy? Her next thought popped right out of her mouth. "Awesome! He's incredible."

Just as Cindy looked up, Grant was lifting himself into a low crouch on his surfboard and riding a really enormous wave in toward the shore. But Grant didn't seem to care about the rough water. He was smiling as he shifted into a standing position, and as the wave broke behind him, he made keeping his balance look easy.

Cindy had rarely seen a surfer look so good—in more ways than one. Grant's strong muscular body glistened in the spray and sun. Did all surfers from Hawaii look like that? Cindy wondered. Then her hometown pride got rankled. She realized that none of the kids around the local scene were that good. In fact, watching Grant approach the shore, Cindy realized that he was the first kid her age she'd met who really was better than she was.

So Cindy wasn't smiling when Grant tossed his surfboard on the sand, waved at her, and quickly jogged across the beach toward her.

"*When* did you say you met him?" Carey said with an annoyed toss of her head. "Yesterday?" Her brown eyes narrowed as she studied Cindy and looked quickly back toward Grant.

Before Cindy could reply, Grant ran up.

"Water's rough today!" he announced, slipping

his sunglasses down off his eyes. He didn't seem to notice the other girls, but singled out Cindy and greeted her with a warm smile.

"Didn't seem to bother you much," Cindy said a trifle sharply. She stretched her arms above her head, then bobbed down over her toes. She didn't look Grant in the eye as she said somewhat reluctantly, "You looked pretty good out there. Tell me, are the waves always that big in Hawaii?"

"Heck no." Grant laughed and bent over to one side to knock the water out of his ear. When he stood up again, he looked Cindy directly in the eye and said with a deadpan expression on his face, "They're usually bigger."

"Hey, MacPhearson," Duffy called as he strode up, followed by Joey Marvel and Tom Patnick. "You were out of sight. That was a regular tidal wave you rode in, man. Did you see him, Cindy? He's going to be great for the Surfing Club."

"You *are* going to join the club, aren't you? I mean, we need a guy like you on the team. No one, but no one, has gone into the water yet today. It's so rough out there," Carey cooed, making Cindy want to throw up.

What was the matter with everyone, anyway? Didn't they have any pride? Without saying another word, Cindy tore off her dad's old denim workshirt, grabbed her surfboard, and ran headlong toward the water.

"Hey, watch it. It's really rough out there," Grant called after Cindy. A look of real concern crossed his face as he turned quickly to Duffy. "I'm not kidding. I almost went under for real beyond the breakers."

"Don't worry," Cindy shouted back over her shoulder as she paused a minute before plunging into the water. "I can take care of myself."

But her words were lost in the roar of the surf.

Only a little ways from shore, Cindy was pretty sure that she had never experienced such rough surf. Maybe Grant was simply bigger and stronger than she was, but fighting her way out beyond the breakers seemed nearly impossible. "If he can do it, I can," Cindy muttered, and paddled determinedly out into the swells.

Even beyond the breakers the water was choppy and colder than usual for this time of year. Cindy wished she had worn a wet suit. She forced herself to concentrate on the water, on the swells surging toward her, and not on the crowd she knew was watching her from the beach. Finally she spotted the wave she'd been waiting for. She began paddling furiously, and her timing was perfect. She lay low on the board and, at the right moment, began rising into a low crouch, but her heart caught in her throat. Maybe she had made a big mistake. The water was so rough that the board vibrated like crazy beneath her, and it took all of her concentration not to fall. Willing her shaking knees steady, she stood up and held out her arms for balance.

The feeling was exhilarating. The spray lashed

at her face, and the keening gulls circling over-head seemed to be cheering her on. The line of distant figures along the beach seemed fuzzy at first, but as she angled her board in toward shore they grew more distinct. She could pick out the kids' brightly colored suits and even Winston's blurry black shape looming ahead. She couldn't tell from this distance, but she knew that all eyes were on her—including Grant's. This had to be the biggest wave she'd ever ridden, but it was the best feeling in the world—as if she were flying with wings over the water. A big, broad grin crossed her face. She was going to do it. She was going to show Grant MacPhearson exactly how good kids from Santa Barbara could be.

The giant wave finally flattened out, and Cindy touched down into the foam.

A lot of the kids rushed down the beach toward her. Winston splashed through the water and jumped against Cindy, practically pushing her back into the waves.

"Down, boy!" she sputtered, and pushed her way through the crowd onto the beach.

"Hey, Lewis. That was great!" Duffy yelled as he hugged her, and Joey and Tom slapped her on the shoulder.

Cindy grinned. She was too winded to talk and was grateful when Nicole ran up and handed her a towel.

"You're the craziest sister a girl ever had," Nicole declared, a note of pride in her voice. "But the best. Cindy, that was scary, and you looked so good."

"Good?" Mollie scoffed. "I don't know anything about surfing, but you looked as good as *he* did." She grunted sharply as Nicole poked her in the ribs.

Cindy, pushing herself away from the center of the noisy crowd, shook her hair out and pushed up her sunglasses. Everyone seemed to be talking at once, but their voices were muffled. She had water in her ear, and the sand didn't feel very firm yet under her feet. The sky seemed all swirly and the sun very bright. She actually felt a bit dizzy, and the whole world looked tilted. Now that she was back on dry ground, she was surprised that she had made it without wiping out.

Instinctively she looked around for Grant. He was standing at the edge of the group of kids, a slight frown on his face. Then he caught Cindy watching him, and he smiled, though she could swear his smile didn't look very wide or sincere as he said, "That was a pretty good show, Cindy. It was rough out there. You're quite a pro." But he didn't walk up to her or slap her on the back or tousle her hair like her other friends.

Instead, he slung one arm over Duffy's shoulder, the other over Joey's, and led them further down the beach. While he was still within earshot, he said, "Duncan, it's all in the timing. It's not as hard as it looks. I'll teach you guys how to do it. We've got lots of rough water back home.

You've got to learn a few new tricks. That's all. Any guy can do it."

"I don't believe it," Cindy muttered, angrily shaking the water out of her ear. "He's a rotten loser. That's what he is."

"Loser?" Mollie forced her eyes away from Grant's departing figure and back to Cindy. "He's no loser. I mean, look at him. Anyway, what was the contest?" she asked.

"There was no contest." Cindy shrugged, and began looking for her beach bag. Then she noticed that Carey and Anna were trailing after the guys, listening to every word of Grant's speech, "How to Ride the Big Wave." "It's just that he doesn't want to believe anyone from here could be as good as someone from Hawaii. That's all."

Cindy had strolled away toward her beach towel and located her bag. Planting her feet firmly on the pale sand, she brusquely rubbed more sunblock on her nose.

"Cindy, when you turned up today that guy was obviously interested in you, and now look. He's just up and walked away. I think you hurt his pride. I mean, it was pretty obvious you went into the water just to prove something," Nicole chided.

"To prove she doesn't care if he's interested or not," Mollie said shrewdly. "If you wanted to scare a guy away, you certainly picked the best way to do it."

"Oh, shrimp, won't you shut up?" Cindy groaned

and threw herself down on the sand, closing her eyes and hoping her sisters would go away.

But Mollie, without missing a beat, continued. "For instance, that awful white stuff on your nose. Not even someone's mother would walk around wearing garbage like that on her face in public. What guy could be interested in you looking like that?"

Cindy sat up and shoved her sunglasses up on her head. She glared into Mollie's big blue eyes. "Interested, interested, interested," she mimicked her kid sister's lilting voice. "For your information, all Grant's interested in is showing off. Someone had to show him that we aren't a bunch of nerds. And as for my nose, it's the only way to keep from getting sunburned. I hate peeling red noses. It's bad enough I get freckles."

"That's still no reason to compete that way against a guy." Nicole spread out her towel and dropped down next to Cindy.

"I'm not competing with a guy. I just wanted to show him I'm as good as he is. He thinks he's better than anyone else around here because of where he's from. He's wrong, and I wanted to show him. That's all. Anyway, surfing's a sport, Nicole. And you don't know the first thing about sports. It feels good, exciting, better than anything in the world, to win. Even if you lose, trying to win is worth the whole game. Stick to your art stuff, Nicole. I'll stick to surfing."

With that, Cindy pulled her sunglasses down

over her eyes and angrily began stuffing her gear into her bag.

"Well, I think—" Mollie started.

Cindy bounced to her feet and pulled on her shirt. "I really don't care what you think," she snapped. "I've got homework to do. Collecting sand dollars is more important right now than listening to you two carry on about me and Grant. There's nothing to carry on about, anyway."

With Winston at her heels she marched up the beach, away from her startled sisters, away from the crowd, and toward the marina. Near the high-tide line, Cindy bent down over a hank of sea-weed, searching for sand dollars. She shook out a thick, tangled mass of the blackish stuff. No sand dollars. Just some broken clam shells and some-thing pretty, pink, and scalloped. Usually she'd save the scalloped bits for one of Nicole's col-lages, but today she felt more like hiding the seaweed in her older sister's bed. Cindy toyed with the idea only an instant before tossing the weeds back onto the ground. She wasn't in the mood for practical jokes.

As she headed toward the cove she stopped a moment and, shielding her eyes, stared intently out to sea. To anyone watching her, she would seem to be looking at the row of offshore oil rigs rising like ship masts along the western horizon, but beneath her sunglasses and out of the cor-ners of her eyes she was looking back toward the line of surfers heading out into the waves. Grant, of course, led the way. Duffy and Joey and Carey straggled behind him into the water. Part of her wanted to be there with them—it would be fun to learn some new surfing moves—but part of her wondered why they had no pride.

And another part of her felt left out and confused. Why did she have this feeling that some kind of battle line had just been drawn in the sand? Grant MacPhearson on one side. Cindy Lewis on the other.

Chapter 3

Cindy peered into the mirror and addressed the small gray and white cat daintily picking her way through the trophies on top of the dresser. "Smokey," she declared, "my sunscreen failed me again and I look like an ad for sun-damaged hair! But don't you go tell Mollie on me." Cindy wagged a finger in the cat's face. "She'll say it serves me right. Can't you hear her now? 'I told you so, Cindy Lewis. You scared away Grant and that ugly stuff on your nose still didn't work. Now look at you!' "

Cindy laughed at her impersonation of her kid sister and leaned even closer toward the mirror, gingerly rubbing her nose with her finger. She shrugged and continued. "Smokey, she's going to notice by tomorrow anyway. I predict by break-fast I'll have about a billion more freckles and I'll be peeling—again. Ugh!" She grimaced at her re-flection, then scooped up the cat and turned around to study the mess she had made in clean-ing her room.

Her closet was empty. Her drawers all dusted out.

The rest of the room looked like a tidal wave had swept through it. "Born in the USA" was blaring from somewhere in the vicinity of a backpack and laundry bag, but the stereo was nowhere in sight. But Cindy wasn't looking for the stereo or the phone or even Cinders, the other cat, who had vanished an hour ago in a pile of shoes and boots. Instead, she stared forlornly at her bed.

She surveyed the colorful piles of sweaters, jeans, and T-shirts, and faced the awful fact head-on. On Monday, the professional photogra-pher was scheduled to take photos of all the sophomores for the yearbook. And for the first time in her life Cindy felt as if she had absolutely nothing to wear.

"Bon appétit, maman!" Nicole's musical voice drifted upstairs. Cindy grinned as her sister's phony-sounding French gave way to enthusiastic English. "Wow, these canapes are terrific!" She was in the kitchen helping her mother test reci-pes. Mrs. Lewis's Movable Feasts business oper-ated from a shop in town. But she often tested

new recipes in their kitchen. Taste-testing was one of Cindy's favorite jobs.

Nicole's voice dropped to a whisper, and for a second Cindy thought she was telling their mother about Grant. Cindy would kill her, but then she realized that her sister would never do that. It would be like telling on Mollie and Brett. Cindy frowned at the thought; no it wouldn't. Anyway, there was nothing to tell. As she noisily rolled her skateboard back into the bottom of the closet, Cindy tossed in her hiking boots, roller skates, and a couple of pairs of smelly sneakers.

She pulled her pup tent out from under her desk and hoisted it up onto the closet shelf. Suddenly she felt pretty dumb about spending all her birthday money on this hiking gear. It was almost as stupid as turning down her mother's offer to take her and Nicole on a shopping spree a month before school reopened while Mollie was still off at camp. Nicole had made out like a bandit. Cindy had turned up her nose at the booty: two frilly blouses, one flowered skirt, one black miniskirt, one silly dress that looked like an apron with pockets, and two pairs of tailored pants. She couldn't imagine how many clothes Nicole would wrangle out of her mother next year before she set off for college. But at the moment she wished she had some new clothes of her own.

"Knock, knock." Nicole poked her head into Cindy's room. She was carrying a tray with a cola, a bottle of mineral water, and a plate of something that smelled terrific. "Hungry?"

"Starving!" Cindy declared, surprised that Nicole was offering her food even before commenting on the chaos of her room.

"Thought so. Ugh, what a miserable job for such a nice day. What happened to the expedition for sand dollars?" Nicole asked, clearing a spot on Cindy's dresser for the tray and handing her the cola. She took a quick sip of her mineral water and looked at the half-empty closet and the clothes heaped on the bed. "In fact, cleaning closets is my *bête noire.*"

"Your what?" Cindy managed as she gulped down some cola and reached for what looked like a bite-size pizza that was missing its tomato sauce.

"My thingIhatemostinthewholeworld. That's more or less what it means," Nicole explained in a slightly superior tone. "I save closet cleaning for rainy days, myself."

Cindy laughed. "Your closet is always clean. Anyway, I'm not cleaning my closet. I'm cleaning my room."

"What did you do this time?" Nicole gave a knowing laugh.

"Swore a solemn oath to Mom and Dad last night over a midnight snack that I'd get this room in order by dinner today or forfeit my trip to Baja. I'm working off this week's detentions." Cindy paused to consider if she should confide in Nicole. She decided it wasn't worth risking another lecture on Grant and how to catch a guy she had no intention of catching. So she simply explained about the sand dollars and left out the part about wanting to get away from the crowd and being alone. "The sand dollars apparently got wind of Miss Harris's plans. I couldn't find any—whole ones, that is. Part of one is right behind you, near the tray."

Nicole jumped and stared at the dresser. Sure enough, half of some spiny flat purplish creature lay next to the plate of little pies. "That's disgusting." Nicole grabbed the tray and sat down primly on the edge of a chair stacked with tank suits.

"Is not. Once it was alive and very pretty, too," Cindy said with a haughty sniff.

Nevertheless, Nicole eyed the dresser suspiciously and took another sip of mineral water.

Cindy grabbed two more of the little pies off the tray in Nicole's lap. "What are these? They're great."

Nicole frowned and quickly claimed the one small pie left in the plate. "Quiche. Finger-size ones. They will be nice at the cocktail party Mom's catering tonight. Down on the yacht. I wonder what people will wear." She concluded dreamily, "I wish caterer's daughters could go to these things—as guests, not servers, that is."

Cindy unearthed a jumbo bag of potato chips from her desk. "Sorry to hog the quiches. I know there are a couple of Snickers bars around here somewhere. Meanwhile, have some of these." She plunged her hand in.

"I can't. They make my face break out." Nicole, whose clear complexion was one of her chief sources of pride, grimaced. "I don't know how you do it. You never put on a pound, and you're always eating."

"Burn it off, I guess. That's one of the advantages of sports," Cindy said, a slightly defensive edge creeping into her voice. She was sure that any minute now Nicole would launch into a lecture about competitiveness and guys and Grant and surfing.

Instead, Nicole put down her bottle of mineral water and fingered the stack of bathing suits behind her on the chair. "I was thinking of going shopping."

"More clothes?" Cindy exclaimed.

"Just a sweater to go with my new skirt. There's a sale down at the mall. Mom said I could borrow the car." Nicole gave a quick critical look at Cindy's outfit: frayed old cutoffs and a drab green "I Survived Grant Canyon Wilderness Camp" T-shirt. She wrinkled her nose. Cindy must have had that shirt since she was twelve. The white lettering was peeling. Just like Cindy's nose, Nicole thought, and stifled a giggle. She cleared her throat and added casually, "In fact, I was wondering if you felt like buying anything," she asked.

"Can't," Cindy mumbled through a mouth full of chips. "I've spent all my money on this stuff."

She waved her drink toward the closet floor. "But I bet Mollie would jump at the chance. Have you noticed that since the last issue of *Seventeen*, she's only been wearing red—red and black to be exact. Her wardrobe is going to need serious revamping to keep up with this fall's current hot look. Wasn't everything yellow last month? I seem to remember my best yellow hooded sweat shirt being clothes-napped around August tenth."

Nicole grinned. "Tell me about it. Friday she walked off with my red sweater and stretched it beyond recognition. It's Mollie's now. But she can't come, because she never came back from the beach. She was last seen with Linda in hot pursuit of some boys wearing UCSB sweat shirts and heading for the Burger Barn by the lagoon."

Nicole headed for the door. She bit her lip, then turned back toward Cindy. "You know, Mother wouldn't mind if you put some stuff on her charge card. After all, you didn't buy anything for school yet."

Cindy frowned. "Did Mom put you up to this? Just now, downstairs? I heard you two whispering. Were you talking about me and my wardrobe—again?"

Nicole heaved a deep sigh. "No. I just asked her if you could come along with me to buy some stuff. That's all."

Cindy studied her sister's face. Nicole was a crummy liar, and she wasn't lying now, though Cindy had a feeling Nicole had something up her sleeve. "If this is one of your plots to get me to wear a dress—"

Nicole winced, then gave an embarrassed little smile. "I can't help it. Look at your bed. Your entire wardrobe looks like an ad for *Sports Illustrated* and *Runner's World.* It seems to me that a fifteen-year-old girl should have one outfit that looks different from her gym clothes—especially considering yearbook pics are on Monday."

Cindy grunted. She wanted to protest and she started to say no. But a reluctant "Okay" worked its way past her lips. "I'll tag along." Then, to be honest, she added, "Actually, just before you came up I was wishing I had something new for the pictures Monday."

"So let's get going," Nicole said.

"But I've got to be back in time to clean up this mess before dinner—or I don't go to Baja."

"What is all this about Baja?" Nicole asked.

"I'll tell you all about it on the way to the mall—it's got to do with biology and Miss Harris and tube worms."

"Spare me the details." Nicole groaned as they clattered down the stairs and into the front yard.

As Nicole waited to make a left turn into the parking lot of Pete's Pizzeria, Cindy glanced furtively over her shoulder at the parcels in the back of the old Volvo wagon. Only one box belonged to Nicole; the other two were hers.

An hour ago, standing in the dressing room of

the Sand Urchin Boutique, her choice of a slim knee-length denim skirt had made perfect sense. It didn't look too different from wearing blue jeans, but it looked different enough to make Cindy feel she had bought something really new. And the oversized crisp white blouse Nicole passed up had looked terrific against Cindy's tan. She had stood awkwardly staring at herself in the mirror, feeling as if she were a little girl playing dress-up. The idea made her smile, and when she smiled she decided she liked the way she looked. That was the moment Nicole suggested she get a pair of pierce-them-yourself earrings.

But now, eyeing the bikes pulled up at the rack in front of Pete's, Cindy thought she must have been delirious. She's never cared about clothes before. They were only something useful to put on your back, help you run, hike, or swim more comfortably. Whatever had gotten into her? Wait until Carey and Anna saw her in a skirt. Ever since she was eight years old she had flatly refused to wear skirts and dresses. And how could she ever keep a white cotton blouse looking all clean and white? Within an hour of putting it on she'd look like the "before" picture in a bleach commercial.

It was too late now. The clothes, on sale, had been marked "nonreturnable." So were the earrings.

"Looks like half the school's here!" Nicole commented as she climbed out of the car.

Cindy, tugging down the back of her frayed cutoffs, took a deep breath. She felt pretty weird about having stomped away from her friends this morning after Grant had more or less led everyone off for his surfing demo. She wasn't used to being on the outside of any crowd. Not that anyone had excluded her. She had excluded herself. But Grant hadn't asked her to come along either.

Not that she blamed him, exactly. Actually the more she thought about it, the more sense it made that he wasn't too enthusiastic about her performance in the surf. After all, Grant was the new kid in town eager to prove himself. He wanted to fit in. In his shoes she'd feel exactly the same way and probably come on a little strong about her surfing. Now she felt guilty. Just when everyone had been congratulating him she had elbowed in and stolen his thunder.

Had she thought about it first, she wouldn't have challenged him like that—so fast. She could kick herself. She could have hung around a while longer before braving the waters. Of course, come to think of it, had her head been at all screwed on this morning, she probably wouldn't have gone out surfing at all. She had committed a cardinal sin of surfing. The conditions were too rough for her. And she had known it when she was paddling out beyond the breakers. She was lucky she hadn't wiped out and gotten really hurt, but as usual she had acted without thinking first.

Well, next time she ran into him, she'd be sure to walk right up to him and tell him how great he had looked—maybe she'd even ask him for some pointers, although she was pretty sure she didn't need them.

As she pushed through the door of Pete's a blast of music and the smell of tomatoes, onions, and sausage hit her in the face.

"Hey, Cindy, where's our champ been all day?" Joey called out from a table by the window. "Hi, Nicole."

Cindy didn't know what to say until she remembered she had a perfectly valid excuse. "Homework. Looking for sand dollars. Harris gave us a crazy paper to do by Monday."

A chorus of groans met her announcement. "Don't tell me about it!" Duffy complained. "Our lab section has to find some exotic sort of sea urchin that I swear only grows off the coast of Maine. But it's Saturday. I don't want to think about school. You should have stuck around."

Cindy shrugged sheepishly and deposited herself in the next booth. Nicole threw her bag down on the seat and went to the counter to order. Then Cindy noticed her friend Anna. She was smiling in a silly spaced-out way that meant she was trying to keep a big secret. She was sitting in the corner of the crowd's booth, sandwiched between the window and Duffy, whose arm was slung across the back of the seat. His freckled fingers drummed the orange plastic seat cover, just inches from Anna's thick long hair.

She looked directly at Anna as she replied, "I

guess I should've. I'm sure I missed something."
Anna blushed and quickly stared out the window.

"You sure did." Carey's blond head popped up
over the back of the booth. "I mean, no one, but
no one, had any luck today. You and Grant were
the only ones who didn't wipe out."

Carey motioned across the floor. Grant was
walking toward the booth, carrying a Pete's Pep-
peroni and Pepper Super Deluxe Special. "Admit
it, Grant," Carey taunted with a toss of her thick
blond braid. "Cindy's one of the best surfers you've
ever seen."

Cindy shifted uneasily in her seat. She hadn't
expected to see Grant so soon. There were too
many people around for her to start telling him
how great he looked this morning. Anyway Cindy
didn't think she could fake the line about getting
some pointers. Especially with Duffy watching. So
Cindy just looked Grant directly in the eye and
said, "Hi, Grant," in a normal, friendly tone of
voice, though she was feeling anything but normal.

As he looked at her Cindy's heart skipped a
beat, and suddenly she knew that Nicole had
been right. Grant looked hurt and uncomfortable.
Her first impulse was to jump up, grab his arm,
and say, "Hey, it's okay. You're a good surfer and
so am I. Welcome to the club." Or something like
that. Except Cindy found herself tongue-tied. She
just looked at him and leaned back against the
window and grinned a silly grin. The hurt expres-

sion vanished from his face, and his sparkling eyes turned cold as ice and very distant.

That's when Cindy knew that the battle lines she felt this morning weren't just written in the sand. They were carved in stone. And Cindy had no idea how to erase them.

Grant put down the pizza and threw up his hands in a gesture of mock surrender. "I admit it. She's pretty good."

"Come off it, Grant!" Duffy chided. "Cindy's great and you know it."

"She's not bad for a girl!" he added, winking broadly at Cindy.

Cindy couldn't believe what he had just said. "For a girl?" she heard herself responding shrilly.

Nicole walked up, holding a small pizza, and whispered, "Cindy, what's going on?"

"Grant just insulted me, that's all," she grumbled, lowering her voice and ripping a wedge off the pizza.

Joey's raucous laugh burst out over the room. "MacPhearson, you've got to admit that Cindy's as good as you are, even if she is a girl."

"In fact," Carey cried gleefully, "you might say you're not bad for a guy either."

"Not bad?" Grant mumbled. "Thanks."

Amidst some arguing about the relative worth of girls and boys, Joey suddenly caught everyone's attention. "I've got a great idea. Let's find out who's better. Girls or boys. Cindy or Grant."

"How?" Duffy asked as Grant leaned forward.

"A contest. A surfing contest," Joey explained. "We could hold it at the Big Luau next week."

While Cindy and Grant exchanged startled glances, all the kids started talking at once.

"Right, Grant, so what of it?" Duffy finally leaned forward, staring intently at Grant.

"Well," he mumbled, looking from face to face at the excited kids all around him. For a second Cindy thought he was going to decline—which was exactly what she wanted to do.

But then Joey piped up again. "Afraid Cindy will win?"

Nicole shot a withering glance at Joey and, turning to Cindy, said quickly under her breath, "Don't do it."

But before Cindy could think, she heard Grant saying, "Of course not. It's a great idea. We can settle this thing once and for all. That is, if Cindy's not afraid of losing."

And then Cindy heard herself saying, "You bet." *Grant* certainly didn't look afraid of losing.

Grant stood back, surveying the excited crowd. It seemed as if everyone had jumped up and was slamming Cindy on the back or pumping her hand. Cindy, caught up in all the attention, started to laugh, but Grant didn't know that it was out of nervousness.

Then he spoke up. "Hold it, folks."

"Are you going to back down?" Duffy asked.

Grant glared at Duffy and growled, "No way, Duncan. I'm just wondering who's going to judge this." Grant gave a meaningful glance at the beach set gathered in the pizzeria. "Where are we going to get nonpartisan judges? It seems to me Cindy may have a bit of an advantage here." He folded his arms across his chest and tapped his foot.

Cindy defiantly planted her hands on her hips. "What you mean is you want some of your macho Hawaii buddies to be the judges."

"No." Grant laughed easily. "Just not anyone from your crowd. People from the swim team in school. Seniors, maybe. Can you arrange that? Can you speak to the captain of the swim team?" He turned to Duffy, as if he were the leader of the group.

"I can," Cindy spoke up sharply. "Because *I'm* captain of the swim team." She paused, letting her words sink in. "I certainly can find a very good group of judges. And they'll be absolutely nonpartisan. Six judges—three girls, three guys. All seniors, so they aren't in either of our classes."

Grant gave a formal, apologetic bow. His whole attitude suddenly seemed mocking. If they had both been ten years old, Cindy would have punched him. As it was, it was pretty hard restraining herself now. At the same time she felt hurt. She had hoped that he liked her and would be a friend.

"Good!" Grant raised his voice enough to be heard over the din. He held Cindy's glance one long instant. "And may the best man win."

"You mean, *best person!*" Anna corrected vehemently. At that moment Cindy wanted to hug her; instead, she forgave Anna for not caring about the Dodgers. She forgave Anna her dumb crush on Duffy. She even forgave Anna her skimpy new bikini, and she simply flashed her best friend her biggest smile.

Grant, his arms still folded across his chest, seemed to be looking directly at Cindy, sizing her up. At that moment Cindy almost hated him. She'd show him at the luau.

But Duffy pulled her over beside him. He slung one arm around Grant and one arm around her. Cindy's head was reeling as everyone began talking all at once—about the time of the contest, the tide, the fact that there would be a full moon.

Only Nicole sat alone, shaking her head, watching Grant watch Cindy. She could swear he was interested in her sister, but just as Mollie said, the way things looked now, Cindy was going to blow her chances with a really great-looking guy who, with just the right encouragement, would fall head over heels in love with her.

Chapter 4

*M*ollie lay facedown on the living room carpet, waiting for Sarah to pick up the phone. She glanced out the window at the rain, which was still coming down hard. So much for finding those guys down at the marina today. But at least rainy Sundays were good for phone calls. And she had plenty to talk about.

She thumbed through her address book. So far she had spoken to Linda, Arlene, Maureen MacNamara, and Mandy Schafer. The only person left after Sarah was Margie Waxman from Algebra I. Except she didn't have Margie's phone number yet. Maybe Sarah had it. Where was Sarah, anyway? The phone must have rung a zillion times.

Kicking her feet up in the air, she idly fingered

the array of candy bars lined up in front of her: one Snickers, one Nestlé's Crunch, two Butterfingers, and a cellophane-wrapped peppermint stick. Just as her hand settled on the peppermint stick, Sarah answered the phone.

"Sarah, where were you? I almost hung up— It's me, Mollie— You won't believe it— No, I didn't make it through Day Three of the Banana Diet. In fact, I only managed Day One and one-third, so to speak. But tomorrow's Monday and I'll start again— I know, I know—but wait till you hear this! It's the wildest story I've ever heard. And it's *so* romantic!"

Mollie paused dramatically and unwrapped the green-and-pink striped peppermint stick and dunked it into her can of soda. Then she continued, "Remember that a guy that I told you about is head over heels in love with my sister Cindy—yeah, the guy with those killer eyes and muscles— You know the Big Luau coming up Friday?— Stop it, Sarah. I *am* getting to the point." Mollie licked the soda off the end of the candy stick. "He and Cindy are going to have a real live surfing contest— No, I don't know exactly what it means, judges or something like that, but I think"—Mollie glanced up toward the ceiling and Cindy's room and lowered her voice to a whisper—"it means he really likes her. That's what Nicole thinks. I can tell. She's worried about Cindy, but I read just the other day that sixteen-year-old guys do dumb showoff things to impress a girl they like. Oh, you read it too? Anyway, do you believe it? I bet the whole school's going to take sides. Boys against girls— No, Cindy was *not* dumb; I think it was smart. It shows she likes him."

"Mollie, how long are you going to hog the phone!" Nicole yelled from the kitchen. "I'm going to tell Mother if you don't get off. I've got a date with Mark tonight, and he's supposed to be calling any minute." Nicole walked through the door in time to hear Mollie ask Sarah for Margie Waxman's number.

"No more calls!" Nicole declared, marching up to her sister, but stopped with a horrified little gasp when she spied the assortment of candy bars on the carpet. "And watch your feet. You almost knocked over Mom's crystal giraffe."

"Sorry." Mollie looked up at Nicole and mumbled apologetically, then noisily bit a piece off her peppermint stick. "What'd you say, Sarah? Right, 462-4401. I've got it. She's probably home now. I can't wait to tell her. Yesterday she said her brother might be in Grant's class. I know he's a nerd, but it's the only way to find out all about Grant. Oh, he's so gorgeous. If only Cindy hadn't seen him first— See you later."

Mollie hung up the phone and sat up and hugged her knees to her chest. "Oh, Nicole. Isn't this all too exciting for words?"

"Apparently not. You've been talking about Cindy nonstop for two hours now," Nicole said wryly. "And I think you'd better stop, fast."

"Oh, I won't stay on long with Margie, I promise. I hardly know her yet, but her brother—"

Nicole grabbed the phone from Mollie's hand. "I know. Her brother's in Grant's class. You announced that fact loud enough for the whole neighborhood to hear it." She gave a meaningful glance toward Cindy's room at the top of the stairs.

"Oh!" Mollie's hand flew to her mouth. "I didn't realize . . ." she whispered hoarsely. "But I didn't say anything bad about her, really I didn't."

Nicole closed her eyes and sank down in her father's favorite easy chair. When she opened them, she stared hard at Mollie, and a warm smile spread across her face. Her little sister Mollie was *impossible. L'enfant terrible!* and a hundred other things Nicole didn't know the words for in French yet, but it all boiled down to exasperating.

Nicole took a deep breath and patiently tried to explain. "Mollie. It's not a matter of saying good or bad things, and I'm not going to give you a lecture on gossiping. The point is, Grant is Cindy's business, not yours or mine. And thanks to you, by tomorrow everyone in town is going to know about this stupid contest."

"But it's not stupid. I read that guys who show off like Grant's doing really like a girl," Mollie said solemnly.

Nicole raised her eyebrows and groaned. "Mollie, it's Cindy who's being the showoff. Don't you understand? I mean, it's so obvious. She's trying to compete with him. To show him she's better than he is. That's no way to get a guy. Guys don't want to have a rival for a girl friend."

"Shhh!" Mollie's eyes rolled upward toward the ceiling. "I think I see what you mean," she whispered, and drew closer to Nicole, offering her a piece of candy. Nicole declined. "But I still think it all sounds romantic."

"It's not romantic. Sometimes I think Cindy's hopeless. She hasn't got a romantic bone in her body." Nicole propped her chin on her knees and continued. "But the point is, making such a big fuss about this match is only going to make the whole situation worse. We've got to get Cindy out of this competition. But once everyone in town hears about it, she'll never back down."

"She's too proud for that!" Mollie added just as the phone rang. She grabbed it. And handed it to Nicole. "It's Mark, for you."

Nicole leaped up and headed off to her room. "I'll take it upstairs. Hang up for me, will you?"

Mollie muttered a preoccupied "Sure thing!" and flopped back down on the rug to consider all the angles of Nicole's argument. Yes, she could see Nicole's point. Especially that part about a guy's not wanting to have a rival as a girl friend. But she still thought the idea of a competition was romantic. And she was beginning to get a pretty good idea of how Cindy could work the match against Grant to her advantage. Nicole might be right about Cindy competing *against* Grant, but she was dead wrong about Cindy dropping out of the meet.

Mollie sat up and ripped the wrapper off her Mounds bar. She knew exactly what Cindy would have to do the night of the Big Luau. The hard part was figuring out how to convince her stubborn sister to do it.

"Smells yummy! Can I lick the bowl?" Mollie poked her head into the kitchen. Cindy had just put her one and only specialty—double chocolate nut brownies—into the oven. A thick fragrant chocolaty smell filled the room.

"Hey, watch it. You can have half. The rest's for me." With her finger, Cindy drew a jagged dividing line roughly down the middle of the bowl. "Anyway, what happened to your diet? These aren't banana brownies, you know," she teased.

"It's off for the weekend. Beside, I found a new diet. You eat grapefruit Monday and I don't remember what Tuesday, but each day of the week something different. I'll start tomorrow." She spun around on the chair in front of the counter, and after two or three spoonfuls of batter said casually, "You know, Nicole thinks Friday's competition between you and Grant is all wrong."

"Tell me about it," Cindy groaned. "If I hear one more word out of her, I'm going to stuff seaweed in her bedroom slippers."

Mollie giggled. "That would serve her right. Sometimes she thinks she knows it all."

Cindy grinned. "You know, shrimp, sometimes you're okay. You're really okay."

That was the opening Mollie had been waiting for. "Yeah, I think the competition is the smartest thing you could possibly do if you want to get Grant."

"You do?" Cindy said, then added quickly, "But I'm not interested in 'getting' that MacPhearson guy, or haven't you gotten the message?"

"I know, I know." Mollie smiled knowingly at Cindy. "I know that's what you keep saying. But don't you see; the Big Luau is the perfect opportunity. I can see it all now."

Mollie leaped off the stool and struck a dramatic pose. "You paddle out to sea. Far, far beyond the breakers. The moon is full. I checked that already on the calendar. You couldn't have picked a more romantic night for an—an assignment."

Cindy burst out laughing. "I think you mean an assignation."

"Yes, that's it. An assignation." Mollie pretended to be looking behind her at something. "You are lying there on your surfboard just waiting for the right wave. You wait for the really big one, you start riding it in. Then *whammo*. You drown!"

"I *what*?" Cindy gasped in horror.

"Don't be silly, Cindy. You don't *really* drown. You pretend to drown. You've taken enough life-saving courses to know all about drowning. You go under three times like this!" Mollie held her nose and dropped to her knees with a thud. She waved her other hand wildly above her head. Then sprang up. She dropped down again. This time Winston came bounding out of the study and knocked her flat on the floor, licking her face.

Cindy doubled over with laughter. "Mollie Lewis, you really are a little actress! You've even got Winston convinced you need saving."

"Winston, stop it!" Mollie screeched, pushing the huge dog off her chest. "I'm drowning in your affections, you dopey dog." Winston obediently stopped slobbering and backed off and lay at Cindy's feet. Mollie caught her breath and smiled triumphantly at Cindy, who was still chuckling as she peered in the oven at her brownies. "So you like my plan. Admit it!" Mollie clapped her hands gleefully.

"What plan? That I pretend to drown?"

"Really, Cindy, you are so slow sometimes." Mollie groaned. "Pretending to drown is only the first part. Grant jumping in the water to rescue you is the second—and best—part. Presto, you become a twosome. Just like that." She snapped her fingers. "Isn't it a great plan? I thought it up myself."

Cindy stood speechless a second. "Let me see if I've got this right." She started in a slow, deliberate voice. "You expect me to put on an act. In other words, to rig the competition, so that, number one, Grant gets to save me, and at the same time, of course, gets to win. Right?"

Oblivious to the sarcasm in Cindy's voice, Mollie nodded a vigorous yes. "Except I forgot that he would win by default. I mean, that makes it even better, doesn't it?"

"Better!" Cindy roared. "I've never heard anything so underhanded, dumb, and insulting in my whole life. Everyone is crazy. First, Grant puts me down because I'm a girl." Cindy stormed back and forth in front of the stove, waving her pot holder in Mollie's face. "Now Nicole is trying to tell me that I'm the dumbest person in the world for accepting a challenge I can in no way honorably turn down. And you—you—why, Mollie Lewis, I never thought you'd be so sneaky—so dishonest!"

"Whoa," Mollie gasped, and jumped to her feet. "I'm not being sneaky or dishonest. I just gave you a reasonable suggestion as to how to catch a guy. If you're not interested, don't take my advice. That's all," Mollie said huffily.

"You don't catch guys. You catch fish. And colds. And all sorts of other things, but how many times do I have to tell you? I'm not interested in Grant MacPhearson that way."

"A million times. You could tell me a million times, Cindy, and I wouldn't believe it. You think you're different from everyone else. But you're not. You're just stuck-up." Mollie's voice rose. "Even your dumb friend Anna Banana's got a boyfriend now. Everyone saw her and Duffy holding hands on the beach yesterday. What makes you any different?" Mollie glared at Cindy, and a wicked gleam came into her eye. "But then," she added coolly, "if *you're* really not interested, I know someone who is. *Very* interested."

"What? Hands off, Mollie," Cindy blurted out, and felt her face suddenly go all red.

Mollie bit her lip and grinned. "I knew it. You do like him. You do. So much for all your honesty, Cindy," she gloated.

"You little creep. I'm going to kill you," Cindy bellowed.

"Hey, crew, why don't you pipe down. I'm trying to read the paper. Hmmm, those smell good." Mr. Lewis walked into the room. He poked his glasses up on his nose, opened the oven, and eyed the brownies. Then he glanced from Mollie to Cindy. "So what's wrong here?"

"Nothing!" both girls declared stonily.

"Ah, yes. Nothing can be pretty noisy at times. Try to keep it down."

"Don't worry, Dad," Cindy grumbled. "I'm going out for a run. And if one crumb of those brownies is gone when I get back, I'm going to kill a certain obnoxious fourteen-year-old who should learn to stick to her own diets and mind her own business." With that Cindy flounced into the back hall, yanked her short yellow slicker off the rack, and slammed her way out the door into the rain.

Mollie flashed a wide innocent smile at her father and shrugged sheepishly. "Beats me. Must be an attack of that sophomore slump."

Mr. Lewis watched Cindy vanish into the fog at the end of the driveway. Then with a conspiratorial wink at Mollie, he took the brownies out of the oven and pulled a knife out of the drawer. He cut two small squares out of the pan of hot brownies and settled himself down at the counter, while Mollie, stifling a giggle, reached in the refrigerator for the milk.

Chapter 5

"*O uch*," Cindy yelped. "*Carey, you promised
it wouldn't hurt!*"

Cindy and her friends were gathered in Cindy's
room, devouring three-quarters of a pan of brownies and attending to the major operation of piercing Cindy's ears.

"And *you* promised you wouldn't move. Do you
want holes in your ears, or slits?" Carey grumbled,
dabbing Cindy's right ear with a cotton ball soaked
in alcohol. "I still think we should put two holes
in each ear at the same time. Saves trouble later."

Cindy glared mutely at her friend, who expertly
fastened the back of the tiny gold earring. She
proffered her left ear and bit her lip. This time
she managed not to scream, but it still hurt.

"Whoever started the rumor that earlobes have no feelings? Mine are definitely sensitive creatures," Cindy grumbled, and reached for the last brownie. "I don't know why I ever listened to Nicole and bought these to begin with."

Laura Fielding unfolded herself from a shoulder stand and glanced at Cindy. "I think they look great. You look really pretty, Cindy. I'm just not sure why you did it now. I mean, won't they get infected, Carey, what with swimming and all?"

"Nope. Mine didn't. Just put peroxide on them every time you come out of the pool," Carey stated. "And I think it's good she did it now. Yearbook pics and all. I bet there might even be some publicity shots in *Viewpoint* this week."

"There's no match coming up," Cindy said, reaching over to change the record on her stereo. She glanced quickly in the mirror. The tiny gold earrings did look pretty.

"No match!!!" Anna, Carey, and Laura gasped in unison.

"Oh, you mean *that*," Cindy said disconsolately, kicking her bare foot against the base of the white captain's bed. "I don't know what possessed Grant to challenge me like that." She flopped down on her back and stared at the ceiling.

Carey and Anna exchanged smiles.

Laura shrugged. "Whatever, he's sure made a big mistake. After all, yesterday you looked even better than he did, and the surf Friday probably won't be as rough unless another storm's brewing. And you know the waves here. He doesn't. I think he's crazy."

"I don't." Anna shook her head. "He's just trying to be part of the scene, that's all."

"Yeah, even if he loses, he'll make a big splash." Carey giggled. "Everyone in town will know who he is."

"*If* he loses?" Cindy sat up and tossed a pillow at Carey's blond head. "Hey, you're supposed to be my friends, and you act like he has a chance of winning. You're supposed to be on my side."

"We are. But he's good too," Anna said pragmatically.

"If he didn't stand a chance of beating you, it would be no contest," Carey declared, propping the pillow under her head and trying to copy one of Laura's shoulder stands.

"That's true," Cindy admitted. "And I don't exactly mind myself—it's what everyone else thinks."

"What everyone else thinks!" Laura whistled. "Since when do you care about that?"

"Since Grant MacPhearson came to town," Carey declared snidely.

"Hey, what's that supposed to mean?" Cindy frowned. Had Grant's turning up really changed her somehow? She looked again at the earrings, then thought of the skirt and blouse hanging in the closet. She knew all about yearbook pics on Friday, and new clothes had been the furthest thing from her mind. Saturday after Grant had given her the cold shoulder on the beach—that's when she decided she had no clothes.

"Anna's just hung up on romance this week," Laura teased.

"Tell me about it." Cindy giggled, then grimaced. "So are my sisters!" Before anyone could respond, Cindy asked, "Tell me, Carey, how do you deal with your sister? Aren't they the pits?"

"Really. What are yours up to now?"

"They want me to drop out. Or rather *Nicole* wants me to drop out." Cindy stopped herself from revealing Mollie's plan. If by any chance she did lose to Grant, then the rumor might get around that she'd rigged the competition.

"Drop out!" Anna exclaimed. "That would be awful. I mean, the honor of all us girls is at stake!" she said earnestly.

"I know, I know." Cindy threw up her hands in disgust. "But Nicole doesn't understand that sort of thing. I think she lives on another planet."

"In another time zone!" Laura commented just as the phone rang.

Mollie yelled from the hall, "Cindy. It's for you." She opened Cindy's door and gave a silly wave at the group gathered on the floor, then announced dramatically, "It's a guy!"

"So?" Cindy shrugged and walked out into the hall.

"And it's not Duffy! Or Joey!" Mollie said in a loud, singsong voice before flouncing back to her own room.

Cindy picked up the receiver. "Hi."

"Hi, is this Cindy?"

"Yeah. Who's this?" Cindy frowned. She didn't recognize the deep voice on the other end, though it was strangely familiar.

"It's me—Grant. Grant MacPhearson."

"Grant!" Cindy exclaimed, then clapped her hand over her mouth. Luckily her stereo was turned up high. Inside her room the conversation seemed to have turned toward last summer's whitewater race. Laura was giggling while recounting the story of an overturned raft. Cindy quietly pulled her door shut. Down the hall she could hear the shower. Nicole was getting ready for her date. To her surprise, Mollie's door was shut.

Still, Cindy lowered her voice. "How'd you get my number?" She twiddled the phone cord and paced back and forth on the hall carpet.

"Duffy gave it to me."

"Oh," Cindy said. The silence suddenly felt awkward. "Well, why'd you call?" she asked quickly.

"Oh, well. I just wanted to apologize."

"Apologize?" Cindy practically choked. "Why? I mean, what for?"

"Well, for the contest. It was a stupid idea, and if you want to back down, there'll be no hard feelings. I never thought it would turn into such a big thing," Grant stammered. "I thought it would just be a couple of kids down on the beach. It's getting bigger than that," he added forlornly.

Cindy closed her eyes and leaned back against

the wall. With one finger she traced a design on the top of the hall table. Yeah, it had turned into a big thing, she said to herself. Aloud, she repeated, "I know what you mean. It's kind of mushroomed."

There was silence on the other end of the phone. Cindy kept her eyes closed and tried to picture Grant. Those blue-green eyes, that dark, almost black, hair. His glistening white smile. Except he didn't sound as if he was smiling. He sounded different. But she didn't know him well enough to know how he looked when he cleared his throat and began to speak.

"So do you want to think about it? I mean, calling it off."

"Calling it off?" Cindy repeated dreamily, then heard herself. She stood up straight, opened her eyes, and looked directly at the Vista High pennant tacked to the outside of her door. "You want *me* to call it off? That's not fair. Why don't *you* call it off?" And then, before she could stop herself, she added, "I'm not afraid."

Grant's voice suddenly rose slightly. "*I'm* not going to call it off. I just thought you might want to. What are you trying to prove, anyway?"

"What am *I* trying to prove?" Cindy's cheeks flushed. "You started all this!" she sputtered.

"Well, good luck, then, finishing it. Because you're going to need it," Grant growled, and abruptly hung up.

Cindy slammed down the phone and marched into her room.

"Do you know who that was? Do you have any idea?" she challenged her startled-looking friends.

Everyone shook her head no.

"It was that—that—creep. MacPhearson. Do you know what he had the nerve to do?"

"Ask you on a date!" Anna replied promptly. Everyone but Cindy dissolved in giggles.

"Anna, you're nuts. Bananas. Insane." Cindy glared. "You're getting to be as bad as Mollie."

"Sorry. I deserved that," Anna said, duly chastened. "What did he want?"

"Me to quit. To call off the meet." Cindy stared at each girl in turn and stood in the doorway, hands on her hips.

"Unbelievable!" cried Anna.

"He *what*!" said Laura.

"Of all the nerve," growled Carey.

Anna added, "And you? I mean what did you say?"

"What do you think I said?" Cindy's shoulders sagged, and she flopped down beside her desk and twiddled the fringe on her old rag rug. "I told him he was crazy. Or something like that." She ran her fingers through her hair and looked up at her friends. "I told him *I* wouldn't back down. No, not at all." She shook her head. Suddenly she felt scared and a little sad. Had she really been dumb? Grant had just given her a way out of this crazy situation, and she'd passed it up. The sad part was that when he had called her, he had sounded so nice at first on the phone. But, she reminded herself, he had only called to ask her to quit.

There was only a second's silence before her three friends started talking all at once. "Cindy, you're the best. Someone has to uphold the honor of us girls. You're the one to do it," Laura congratulated.

Anna jumped up and hugged her.

Carey just beamed at her from across the room. "And don't you ever think that we aren't rooting for you all the way on this one, Cindy Lewis. Right down to the bitter end."

Chapter 6

*T*he monthly music assembly had just let out, and the lunchroom was packed with students. The line snaked behind Cindy into the hall, past the vending machines, and as far as the front doors.

"For pete's sake!" Cindy exclaimed as she stood in line talking to her friends. "A girl I don't even know came up to me last period and told me good luck. I didn't know what she was talking about until she mentioned Grant. This is getting out of control."

Laura pushed back a stray strand of her long brown hair and tore open a bag of peanuts with her teeth. "If you think that's bad, Cindy, wait until you get in the cafeteria."

"Why?"

Anna, on tiptoe, peered into the cafeteria. "What's wrong?— Oh. Maybe we should skip lunch."

"Why? What's going on?" Cindy looked in. At first nothing seemed unusual; then she noticed that all of the water polo players, swimmers, and surfers were hogging two tables—all of the male members, that is.

Cindy let out a nervous laugh. Nearby, a couple of tables, filled only with girls, were talking animatedly. The two segregated groups seemed charged with excitement, and Cindy had a funny feeling that she and Grant were the reasons for all the excitement.

Cindy couldn't figure out how a simple contest had mushroomed into a major sports event around the school. Even kids who'd never followed any varsity sports were arguing over who would win the meet. As Laura had predicted on Sunday, the school paper had wanted an interview. That's why Cindy was in a skirt again today. The staff reporter—a junior girl with a name Cindy couldn't pronounce—had asked her to be sure to wear something "not too sporty" for the newspaper photo. "We want to play up the girl-versus-boy battle of the sexes angle real big."

Cindy should have given a flat no to both the idea of the interview and wearing the skirt, but suddenly she felt as if it wasn't her match against Grant anymore. It had become girls versus boys, and Cindy, caught up in something bigger than herself, couldn't stop it even if she wanted to. It was like being carried toward shore on the back of a big wave. She had impulsively made the decision to ride in it, and now the force of the water would keep her plunging ahead.

Cindy gnawed the inside of her lip, closed her eyes, and tried to get her stomach to settle down. She'd die before admitting it to Nicole, but more than anything in the world she did want to back out. At least the part of her that was convinced Nicole was right about Grant wanted to quit. Since the weekend, Grant had been playing some kind of distancing act.

During the assembly, Grant had been sitting two rows behind her. When the music was finally over Cindy had turned around to grab her jacket from the back of the chair. She saw Grant and flashed him a friendly smile. He pretended not to see her and looked right past her shoulder and left by the back door—just so he didn't have to say hello. Cindy was sure of that. Now that he regarded her as an opponent, he didn't want her as a friend.

Of course, another part of her didn't want to back out of the competition at all. More than anything in the world, part of Cindy wanted to win—and win big. Sure, all the commotion over the match scared her, but as an athlete, she was used to feeling nervous before a match. And since it seemed that all the girls at Vista were counting on Cindy to defend their honor, she certainly didn't want to let them down.

Nevertheless, she hesitated in the doorway of the cafeteria. Facing Grant on the beach was one thing. Facing him here was something else. Maybe they should head to Taco Rio and eat there. Then she spied Mr. Marshall, the principal, a few feet in front of her in line and muttered, "No way to head out to Pete's or the Taco Rio. Not with Marshall on the prowl. What's he doing here anyway?" she whispered to Laura.

"Displaying the culinary delights of our cafeteria to the string quartet," Laura quipped. Sure enough, the first violinist was craning her neck trying to get a glimpse of the salads, while the cellist sniffed the air and eyed the hot food table skeptically.

Cindy wrinkled her nose and sighed dramatically. "Cook Willie's Cool Chili. Oh, *groan.*" She sank weakly against the doorway. Then the line lurched forward. The principal, the four members of the string quartet, and Cindy all entered the room at once.

A ripple of noise started on the girls' side. It grew and spread and changed into sporadic clapping and cheering.

Mr. Marshall ran his hand over his shiny bald head and smiled a small surprised smile at the students. He gestured graciously toward the startled musicians standing behind him. Only then did the principal begin to frown. The cheering students weren't looking at the performers. They were looking just behind them—at Cindy Lewis. A few girls were calling out her name, and they were all looking at her. Cindy turned red as a beet and prayed the floor would open up and swallow her—before Mr. Marshall did.

"Miss Lewis. What exactly is the meaning of this?" Mr. Marshall asked.

"Sorry, Mr. Marshall!" Cindy stammered, then felt Laura prod her from behind. She looked past the principal's beety face and spotted Carey beckoning enthusiastically from one of the tables dominated by girls. Cindy bolted out of line, scampered to Carey's side, and sank down in the chair her friend had saved for her. Everyone at her table was grinning at her. She looked at all the expectant faces of the girls: Laura, Carey, Wendy Morgenstern, Anna, the entire girls' water polo team, and then three or four girls she didn't even know.

A redheaded girl at the table who Cindy vaguely recognized from the cheerleading squad spoke first. "Cindy, I think the MacPhearson/Lewis showdown at the Big Luau's the best thing that ever happened to sports in this school!"

Cindy broke into a slow grin. Pom-pom girls never hung out around the girl athletes at Vista. In fact, Cindy had never met one before. But she thought they'd all be like Mollie. Insanely, hopelessly boy-crazy. Draped around the nearest available linebacker. But the redheaded girl sounded so sincere, and she wasn't within ten yards of a football star.

The surfing contest hadn't even happened yet, and already things were changing. Cindy had never seen so many girls supportive of one cause before. "Maybe you're right!" Cindy suddenly sat up straighter. With a proud toss of her head she stated firmly and a bit too loudly, "And I'm going to do my best to win. For all of us." Then instantly she felt a little silly and wished she had stayed in line and bought some lunch and kept her mouth shut.

"Even Nicole?" Carey whispered, and gave a meaningful glance toward the cashier's stand. Nicole was looking around the room toward Grant's table, which was filled with boys talking loudly about surfing. Her boyfriend, Mark, was there. Seeing Nicole, Mark sprang to his feet and waved to her. Nicole managed a faint smile, and then took a deep breath. She resolutely marched toward Cindy's table.

"Outstanding, Nicole Lewis! I knew secretly you were one of us!" Laura congratulated her, and made room for Nicole and her tray.

Nicole arched her eyebrows and put her tray down with a clatter. Under her breath she grumbled to Cindy, "Well, if you insist on going through with this, you'd better do it right. Here, eat!" She pulled two lunchbags out of her purse and set one in front of a startled-looking Cindy.

"I don't believe this. You made me lunch!" Cindy

sputtered, then laughed and ripped open the brown bag. "Wow, more cute quiches!" Her eyes were dancing with excitement.

"They aren't just cute; they're good for you," Nicole began to lecture.

"Who cares!" Cindy whacked Nicole on the back and grinned broadly. "The point is, you brought them. And you're here—on our side."

"Not exactly," Nicole started, but Cindy looked so happy, she couldn't continue. In response to Cindy's grin she could only smile. "What do you expect? You're my sister!" She shrugged sheepishly, then daintily pulled the wrapper off her straw and, with one wistful sidelong glance across the room at Mark, plunged the striped straw into her mineral water.

Chapter 7

"*There should be a rule against sisters attend-*ing the same school!" Cindy muttered as she pedaled furiously up the steep hill leading toward the park. "Particularly pesky little sisters." Cindy knew she should feel guilty about sneaking away from Mollie after school. But she didn't. Not at all. At the moment she only wished she could ride far enough so that Mollie would never find her again.

All day long, Mollie and at least one of her silly freshman friends had been trailing Cindy, like two incompetent pint-size gumshoes. First to the auditorium. Then to lunch. Just now Mollie had been hanging out in front of Cindy's locker, talking a mile a minute with the reporter from *Viewpoint* and flirting with every guy who happened to walk by. Cindy almost marched up and insisted that whatever Mollie said about her should be off the record. But she couldn't face the reporter again, so she skipped getting her books, her jacket, and tennis racket and sneaked out the side door through the gym to the bike rack. Homework could wait until another day. Getting away from Mollie was top priority.

Goaded on by her annoyance at Mollie, Cindy pedaled even harder. Hugging the shoulder, she tried to pull ahead of a truck slowly chugging by her on the road. She grinned when she reached the crest of the hill just before the big rig. Then she turned up Lemon Lane and into the park entrance. She raced along the straightaway, coasted down a curvy hill, then pumped energetically up the last steep stretch of road leading to the lookout.

By the time she jumped off her bike and threw it in the grass she wasn't angry at Mollie anymore. She held her arms up to the wind. Somewhere nearby something was blooming. The air was warm and sweet and salty with the sea. She threw her head back and smiled, then dropped down onto her favorite rock and stared at the scene below.

Vista High lay to her right: a red-and-white complex of buildings, playing fields, and glossy tarred parking lots. The kids streaming out of the doors looked like dollhouse figures. The school buses were loading up at the main entrance. She watched them circle the drive and pull out onto

Boulvard and Napa. From where she was sitting they looked like toys.

Mollie had probably discovered that Cindy was missing by now. In fact, she had probably rounded up a search party to find her—to find out the latest about the match, and Grant, and what Mollie insisted should have been a blossoming romance.

At the thought of Grant, Cindy turned and looked down at the beach. The waves looked so peaceful. A few surfers had already hit the beach. Grant was probably with them. Cindy squinted, but she couldn't even tell whether the tiny figures were guys or girls.

She wished she didn't care. She had come up here to get away from Mollie and the competition and all the fuss at school. But looking down on the water only reminded her that where she really wanted to be was down on the beach with her surfboard, clowning around with Duffy and the rest of the crowd, as she had only a week ago.

Why was everything changing? She had been happy with her life before Grant had walked into it. Now he was probably hanging around, having the time of his life, out there on the water with *her* friends, while she was sitting alone, feeling left-out, confused, and overwhelmed.

She stared out to sea, toward where the horizon grew all gray and vague. Somewhere far to the west of the grayness was Hawaii. She wondered what it looked like where Grant had grown up. There would be lots of palm trees and big floppy bright flowers and pineapples and girls in hula skirts with leis around their necks, like in airlines commercials. Of course, there would also be miles of pristine beaches. And crashing down on the sand would be waves. Tall, dangerous waves. Each one towering higher than the next. And beyond the waves the turquoise-blue ocean. Empty except for one of those outriggers paddled by five or six guys—each one as dark-haired as Grant. But none so handsome or with such enormous blue-green eyes.

Her daydream was suddenly interrupted by the sound of someone running up the road in her direction. Cindy's body stiffened, and before she could turn around, someone called her name.

"Cindy? Cindy Lewis. Is that you?"

Cindy caught her breath and looked up. It was Grant. He was wearing gray sweat pants with one of those corny "Psychotic State" sweat shirts. She was too surprised to say anything at first. Surprised and embarrassed. She had just been picturing a white canoe full of Grants and presto, he turned up. Very alive. Very real. And very much in the flesh. Cindy gulped and managed a slight smile.

Then she remembered that the last time she had seen him he had snubbed her, so she jumped to her feet, brushed her hands off on her new skirt, and reached for her bike. "Don't worry," she said sharply. "I was just leaving."

Grant's smile faded. "Oh!" he murmured in a disappointed voice. Then he looked out to sea. "Well ... I was just ... Do you come here often?"

"Yeah." Cindy toyed with the streamers dangling from her handlebars. If she had any pride at all, she would get on her bike and leave. But she didn't want to. Not at all.

"Ummm—I guess there are lots of great places around here," Grant mumbled. "I mean to look at." He stuffed his hands in the pockets of his sweat shirt and sat down on a rock. A different rock from the one Cindy had just jumped up from.

"Where do you live?" they both asked at once, and then turned away from each other in awkward silence.

Cindy sank back down to her old place on the cliff. What now? She had a feeling they would sit there—in silence—forever, unless someone said something.

"I live—to answer your question—there!" Cindy pointed to a red-tiled roof barely visible through the palm trees on a hill to the north of the marina.

"I think I live there!" Grant looked down at the streets of Santa Barbara and after a second pointed in the direction of the university. "My dad lucked out and we got a house right off campus. It's pretty big, and he can walk to work."

"Your dad's a teacher?" Cindy realized she didn't know very much about Grant.

"An English lit professor."

"Mine's an architect. It's kind of nice. He works at home most of the time. My mom's Movable Feasts." Cindy giggled at the puzzled expression on Grant's face. Even when he wasn't smiling, the dimple was still there. "That's a catering business."

"Your mom's a caterer? Wow! Invite me to dinner sometime!"

"Okay." Cindy stuck out her hand. "It's a deal."

Grant cocked his head, then took her hand and shook it vigorously. "Set the date." His hand lingered in hers. Long enough for Cindy to decide he had nice strong hands, and his palms weren't sweaty.

Cindy, coloring slightly, finally pulled her hand away and pretended to swat a fly. "Anytime—*after* Friday," she blurted out, then winced.

Grant kicked at some loose stones at the base of the rock. They clattered off the side of the cliff. After a minute he looked up at Cindy. "That's all right," he said. "Aren't we supposed to be in training?"

Cindy nodded, and suddenly the thought of the match made her stomach go funny. Until she had mentioned Friday, she had felt perfectly comfortable with Grant, as if she had always known him. But she had also felt different. Different from how she ever had with Duffy. And thinking about that made her feel uncomfortable again. Cindy pretended to look up the path. She didn't want Grant to see her face right then. She knew she was blushing.

"So, have you got any brothers or sisters?" Grant sounded tense again.

Cindy looked up, frowning. "I keep forgetting; you really are new around here." She shook her head and explained with a little laugh, "I'm part of the Lewis sisters. The middle of the sandwich, so to speak."

Grant leaned back on his hands and nodded. "So am I. Actually, I'm one part of the middle. There are four of us. Danny's in college back at U. Hawaii. Me. My sister Kimberly—a real pain."

"Wait. Don't tell me. I bet she's fourteen."

Grant rolled his eyes. "Thirteen-and-a-half. She trails around after all my friends. I barely have any friends here yet, and she still trails around. I think she's going to steal Duffy's phone number any day now and start making anonymous calls. I wish we had left her back in Hawaii."

Cindy nodded sympathetically. "And who's the other end of the sandwich?"

"Sally. She's six. No complaints in that department."

"Right, she's still cute, and by the time she isn't, you won't be living at home anymore." Cindy smiled, remembering Mollie and wishing that there were ten years and not one-and-a-half years between them. It would be so much nicer to think of her little sister as cute, and not a pain.

"It must have been hard moving in your junior year," Cindy said after a moment's silence.

Grant grimaced. "You don't really want to know!"

"I do, I do," she insisted.

"It's tough. Not that I don't like it here, and I'm making friends. . . ." Grant's voice trailed off.

He suddenly sounded so sad that Cindy wanted to reach out and touch him. To run her fingers through his thick, dark hair. At the thought she began to feel awkward again.

Grant started speaking. "Like I said, I'm making friends. I've met lots of guys, and you—" Grant hesitated, and Cindy looked up quickly. Their eyes met. Grant held her glance a second, then looked away and ran his fingers through his hair. "And, of course, I've met the other girls who hang out down at the beach."

"Did you know Laura was training for the Olympics—track and field?" Cindy suddenly found herself babbling. She could feel her face getting hot again.

"I heard. Duffy told me." Grant jumped up and began to pace back and forth. He looked nervous, and that made Cindy feel nervous. Finally he said, "Want a ride to the beach? We can put your bike in the back."

"Where's your car?"

Grant gestured toward the parking area a little further up the road. Alongside a graffitied trash can was a sleek red Trans Am.

"Awesome." Cindy whistled.

"Well?" he asked.

He was standing so close to her now that Cindy was afraid he was going to put his arm around her—or kiss her. And suddenly she wanted to kiss him. Horrified, she felt her face turning beet red. Closing her eyes, she pictured herself riding down to the beach with Grant. She really wanted to go with him, but she felt so ill at ease. Nicole would know what to do. For that matter, Mollie would probably know. But Cindy definitely didn't.

"No. No, I'd better ride back," she said glumly. Then to cover her embarrassment, she tossed her head and added with a laugh, "Like you said, we're in training."

The smile slowly faded from Grant's face. He stared at Cindy and shook his head. "I don't get it." He felt in the pocket of his sweat shirt for his keys and started up the road. "What's with you, anyway?" he mumbled. "A ride home's no big deal. But you have to make a declaration of independence. What are you trying to prove?"

"Nothing!" Cindy retorted, but Grant was already out of earshot. She shook her head. Guys, once they weren't just guys anymore, were really impossible. Duffy always made sense. Grant never did. Every conversation she'd had with him so far had ended up with some kind of argument, and Cindy was starting to feel that it wasn't all Grant's fault. Obviously, she was a nerd around Grant. She never said what she meant. This puzzled Cindy, because she had always had lots of guy friends. But with Grant everything was different—she was different.

She hopped back on her bike and started coasting slowly down the hill. Halfway down, a car came up behind her. Cindy stopped, straddled her bike, and shielded her eyes from the sun with her hand. Sure enough, it was the red Trans Am. Impulsively, Cindy waved.

But the car just speeded up, and as Cindy watched it go by, her heart sank. Grant hadn't waved back.

Chapter 8

"*T*his has been the most *exciting day of my* whole life!" Mollie declared in a loud voice as Margie Waxman deposited two chili burgers on the table and pulled up a chair.

When the girls arrived at Taco Rio's after school, Mollie had offered to hold the corner table while her friends went to the counter to get the food. Volunteering to sit down and separating herself from the crowd had been a hard decision. Mollie was bursting with news. But sitting down and letting her news wait five more minutes was the only way she could be sure to get the one good seat—the one with the best view of a nearby group of junior and senior guys.

Margie shoved her glasses up her nose and

pondered Mollie. "Did anyone ever tell you, you talk in italics?" she commented.

"I do what?" Mollie blinked.

"Don't pay attention to Margie." Linda giggled. "Since Mrs. Bowden told her she had promise as a writer, she's been talking funny, I think what she means is every other word you say sounds like it's underlined. In other words, you talk too loud, in case you hadn't noticed." Linda gestured over her shoulder toward the nearby guys. They were looking at Mollie and whispering among themselves.

"I have good reason to talk underlined. After everything that's happened. Cindy and Grant are the talk of the school."

"Mollie!" Margie sank down in her seat and peered over the rims of her glasses at the guys. "*Everyone* can hear you," she warned.

Mollie giggled. "I can't help it!" she continued, not lowering her voice at all. "Attracting attention is just part of being a Lewis, I guess. Look at Nicole, and Cindy." At the mention of Cindy's name the guys at the next table fell silent. They looked at one another and then at Mollie. She smiled a catlike smile and pointedly studied her hands. She had wanted them to notice her and they had.

Sarah sighed. "If I look like Nicole Lewis, I'd attract attention too! Do you know that half the guys in my French section signed up for French Club just because your sister is president? She looked so pretty when she talked about the club on Student Activities Day last week."

"She didn't mean *that* sort of attention!" Margie interrupted. "She meant the kind of attention that Cindy gets because she's such a born leader. I wish *I* had a sister like that. Why, she's as brave as Sally Ride!" She fingered her space shuttle looseleaf binder and sighed.

Mollie fluffed her hair with her fingers and shook her head. "You're dead wrong, Margie Waxman. Dead wrong. Sure, Cindy's brave, and lots of kids look up to her. But she's getting the other kind of attention, too."

"You mean from guys?" Linda gasped. "I thought she thought makeup and clothes and all that stuff was dumb."

"Actually the guys I've talked to around school haven't been giving Cindy the kind of attention *I'd* brag about." Margie sniffed.

Mollie paused dramatically, then leaned in closer. "Didn't you notice—the skirt?"

"The skirt?" the three girls echoed.

Mollie nodded solemnly. "*And* the blouse. When did you ever see my sister in a skirt and blouse? And she wore it today too—not just for yearbook pictures on Monday."

Linda mouthed a silent "oh" as Mollie continued. "And you won't believe what she did just now."

Another dramatic pause.

Then Mollie leaned back in her seat and announced, "She thought I didn't see, of course. I was waiting by her locker—we were supposed to ride home together. But she sneaked away, out the door by the gym, and rode off on her bike alone."

Linda dismissed Mollie with a wave of her hand. "So what?"

"Let me finish, will you?" Mollie groaned. "A few minutes later, *he* pulled out of the parking lot in a red Trans Am."

"He?" Margie frowned.

Sarah suddenly caught Mollie's drift. "Grant MacPhearson," she and Mollie said at once.

"He followed her?" Margie was still skeptical. "Maybe he was just going home."

"No. I checked." Mollie dusted some crumbs off her lap. "I ran out and followed him a little ways on my bike. He went up toward the park; then I turned back and found you guys and came here."

"And that's where Cindy went? To the park?" Sarah asked.

"Well, I think so. She's not at home—I called there. And she didn't have her surfboard. And Lookout Point is her favorite spot, besides the beach."

"So there's really something between them," Margie said in an awed voice. "Whoever would have guessed?"

"Wow, but that changes the whole thing, doesn't it?" Linda toyed with her napkin. "I mean about the big Luau. If there really is something between them."

Mollie shrugged. "I don't know for sure—yet. Cindy hasn't come right out and said anything about it." Mollie paused for effect. "But I can tell exactly how she feels. After all, I *am* her sister and I've been watching both of them all week. And the way he *looked* at her in the cafeteria today. He couldn't take his eyes off her. Didn't you notice?" Mollie asked. No one had, so she added one last bit of information. "Still, he did call her the other day, and they talked for ages on the phone."

"He phoned?"

Mollie nodded.

"That clinches it," Sarah said firmly. "A guy doesn't phone a girl unless he's really interested. How romantic!" She sighed. "They started out as enemies, and now look at them."

"Hold it!" Margie cried. "If he's her boyfriend, won't he let her win Friday?"

"No way!" Mollie blurted out. "She'd kill him. She'd disqualify herself first if she thought he'd do that. She's so honest." She parroted Cindy's own argument. "It's not sportsmanlike. And Cindy's very sportsmanlike." Mollie leaned back in her chair and stared dreamily at a travel poster on the pink stuccoed wall. Under the words "Acapulco Delight" a dark-haired man and a woman in a scrap of a bikini were locked in a passionate embrace. Behind them was a cool green stretch of ocean. Riding the crest of the waves were surfers and windsurfers. At their feet was the price: "Only $199.99, Four Days, Three Nights!" Mollie sighed and looked directly at her friends and said, "Of course, if I were in Cindy's shoes—well—"

"Well, what?" asked Linda impatiently.

"I'd take advantage of the situation," Mollie said smugly.

"How?" Margie queried scornfully.

"I'd drown," Mollie announced dramatically; then, looking at her friends' horrified faces, she started giggling. "Oh, you're all too serious. I wouldn't *really* drown. I'd *pretend* to drown. Imagine being rescued by Grant MacPhearson."

"Mollie Lewis!" Linda gasped, and broke into a nervous giggle. "Of all the crazy ideas."

"It's brilliant, Mollie." Margie adjusted her glasses and stared at Mollie and grinned slowly. "I should have thought of it myself."

"But Cindy won't do that, will she?" Sarah asked in a small, worried voice. "Gosh, it would be so tempting. Grant is so unbelievably cute."

Mollie shook her head vehemently. "Of course not. Haven't you been listening? Cindy might have worn a skirt once or twice, and Grant obviously likes her. But she's too sportswomanlike to cheat at a competition."

"I hope so," Sarah said, obviously not concerned. "Well, if she doesn't pretend to drown, she's missing the chance of a lifetime," Margie stated flatly.

Mollie frowned. "Hey, weren't you listening? Cindy wouldn't ever do that kind of thing. I was just telling you what *I* would do. We're sisters, you know, not clones!" Mollie added, nervously glancing over to the next table.

But the guys seemed to be lost in a heated discussion among themselves. Mollie heaved a sigh of relief and turned her attention to the more important business of hearing exactly what Grant MacPhearson had said to Margie's brother in chemistry lab yesterday afternoon.

Chapter 9

*N*icole was on the edge of the parking lot behind Salty Dog's Snack Shack, slipping off her sandals, when the red Trans Am screeched to a halt behind her.

"Hey, watch it!" she cried, and glared at the car. A tall dark male jumped out. It was Grant MacPhearson.

She gasped and for one brief instant looked inside the car, half hoping to find Cindy in the front seat. No such luck.

Nicole had come down to the beach after school with her staff photographer, Allie Reese, to shoot candid pictures for the yearbook. Allie had already begun to work on some "local color." When Grant pulled up, Nicole was on her way to pry the photographer away from an overflowing bright yellow trash can she had wasted half a roll of film on already. The real purpose of the shoot was to capture a sense of the excitement generated by the forthcoming Big Luau, and Cindy and Grant's one-on-one competition. Except Cindy and Grant were the only two surfers nowhere in sight.

In her heart Nicole had prayed that the fact that they were both missing was a good sign— the MacPhearson/Lewis romance might finally be blooming. Now she was face to face with a scowling Grant, and he looked anything but romantic.

Nicole swallowed hard and offered her hand to Grant. "Hi!" she said brightly. "I'm the editor of *Blue Horizons,* the yearbook, and we're taking some pictures." Grant struggled to control his feelings, then mumbled, "Listen, not today. I'm not in the mood for pictures. Wait. Wait until after Friday."

Nicole smiled. "Yes, of course we'll be there too. But we wanted some casual beach scenes before the luau."

Grant just grunted and strode off across the sand.

Nicole stuffed her sandals into her bag and picked her way across the sand, struggling to keep up with Grant. She had suddenly realized that this was her chance to talk to him, alone. Maybe talking to Cindy wouldn't work. She had to explain to Grant that Cindy really liked him. She was just in this crazy habit of competing with all the guys she knew. It didn't mean anything. She had to make him see that and cancel the match. He only needed convincing, and Nicole seldom had trouble convincing boys to do anything she wanted. Stuffing her hands in the pockets of her white sweat shirt, Nicole crossed her fingers and hurried across the beach, trying to avoid the tangled heaps of kelp and seaweed.

Grant had stopped and thrown his shirt down in the sand. He was looking out to sea. Only then did Nicole realize he didn't have his surfboard. He began peeling off his sweat pants, and by the time she caught up with him, he was stripped down to his swim trunks and heading toward the water.

"By the way," she shouted, over the noise of the surf, "my name's Nicole. Nicole Lewis. You know, Cindy's sister," she added with a sweet smile.

Grant spun around and stared her in the eye. "Exactly how many Lewis sisters are there, anyway?" Before Nicole could respond, he continued in an angry voice. "No, don't tell me. I remember now. Three. Well, there might as well be fifty of you. Every time I turn around, one of you is following me. You girls should open a detective agency," he said sarcastically.

"Wait a minute." Nicole put a restraining hand on Grant's arm. "That's not fair. Cindy and I can't help it if Mollie follows you everywhere. You sure can't accuse Cindy of following you—"

Grant interrupted Nicole with a bitter laugh. "You're right. She's the Lewis who avoids me. Now, what exactly does this Lewis want?" He looked Nicole up and down. She was wearing her best white sweat shirt, and her pale yellow skirt whipped about her legs in the strong wind blowing in toward shore.

Nicole's gray-blue eyes narrowed as she stared at Grant. She angrily yanked her windblown hair out of her face and declared, "You are certainly the rudest person I've ever met in my whole life."

"Then you've never met your own sister!" Grant bellowed, and stormed toward the water. He stopped and yelled over his shoulder, "In fact, you can tell her something for me. She is too stubborn to listen to me, but maybe she'll listen to you. When it comes to that surfing competition, it's no holds barred. I'm going to prove to her once and for all that girls can't hold a candle to guys in the sports department. Tell her to learn to sew or cook for her mother's catering business. That's all she's good for. The sooner she learns that, the better!"

"Grant MacPhearson! That's no way to talk about my sister. And she certainly is as good as any guy I've ever seen on a surfboard," Nicole cried, holding her hat on with one hand. Although she refrained from saying exactly how bad Cindy was at cooking and sewing, she added, "And she bakes better brownies than anyone in Santa Barbara." Nicole wanted to say more, but she was too angry and upset. Grant had a point. Cindy would be happier if she'd stop competing against guys, but Nicole would rather die than admit that to Grant. So she fired one parting shot. "And on Friday, you'd better believe there are no holds barred. You're in for a bad surprise, Grant, if you think you're going to win this competition." With a haughty toss of her head, Nicole spun around and began running back toward the lagoon.

"Of all the nerve," she muttered, then shrieked as her ankle got caught in the kelp. As she pitched forward onto the sand, two strong hands grabbed her and pulled her back to her feet. For a dazed second she watched her beloved straw hat skim across the sand and into the surf. Then she looked up at her rescuer.

Grant held her firmly by the arm. "Hey, I'm sorry. Are you all right?" he asked, avoiding her glance. He looked red in the face and very embarrassed.

Nicole was so furious that she gritted her teeth and tried to glare at Grant. But when she saw the confused, sheepish look on his face, suddenly his outburst about girls and Cindy and her mother made sense. Grant didn't hate girls. And he didn't *really* think girls were bad at sports. He probably loved the idea that Cindy was a great athlete. He liked Cindy and wanted to be her friend—her boyfriend—but Cindy's stubborn competitiveness had hurt him.

Still feeling embarrassed about her own outburst, Nicole kept her eyes averted as she mumbled, "The seaweed. I hate it. More than anything in the world. Except sunburns." She glanced up at the bright California sun and shuddered.

"Are you sure you're from the same branch of the Lewis family as Cindy?" Grant looked hard at the fair-skinned Nicole and squinted. He was still holding her arm.

Nicole was speechless only a second, then burst out laughing.

Grant cocked his head. A suspicious look crossed his face as if he thought someone had played a crazy trick on him. But Nicole's lilting laughter was contagious, and suddenly Grant began chuckling.

He held Nicole's arm as she extricated herself from the kelp. "It's hard to believe, but I *am* Cindy's sister. And I hate seaweed and sports and competitions and this whole mess with the luau," Nicole confessed with a smile.

Grant shook his head. "I don't understand. Then why the pictures, and why did you want to talk to me about the luau?"

"You weren't listening!" Nicole tapped him playfully on his arm and explained patiently, "I'm the editor of the yearbook. I've got to get pictures of all the kids." She talked easily as Grant strolled back with her toward the lagoon. He nodded as she continued. "And I didn't want to talk to you about the luau. I wanted to talk to you about—" She broke off. Cindy was heading down the beach directly toward them. With her surfboard under her arm, she was wearing a wet suit and had an old blue scarf tied haphazardly around her head. Nicole grimaced. Her sister couldn't have looked less romantic if she wanted to.

Nicole forced her face into a pleasant smile and said airily, "Here comes Cindy. What a wonderful surprise!" She waved toward her sister. "Cindy, come here. Look who I found."

But Cindy didn't answer. She marched toward Grant and Nicole and, to their amazement, stomped right by them, ignoring them completely. She held her back tall and straight, and an angry red spot burned on each cheek.

"Cindy?" Nicole's words died on her lips. She looked quickly up at Grant. His rugged strong face wore a hurt expression. "Oh, boy," she murmured, and watched her sister head off toward her friends in line in front of the Snack Shack.

If Cindy hadn't seen it with her own eyes, she wouldn't have believed it. It was the kind of gory story Anna told about her own big sister. Stealing guys like that. Right out from under her nose.

Cindy had come back home from Lookout Point feeling pretty low. Grant hadn't waved to her in the car, and Cindy had felt so hurt that she had almost started crying. And Cindy never cried. Except when one of her pets got hurt; or sometimes when she made one of her sisters cry, she'd storm off to her room, slam the door, and burst into tears because she felt like she was such a crummy person hurting people she loved. But she didn't feel that way often, because most of the scraps with her sisters were the kinds of things that blew over quickly and had nothing to do with being mean or crummy.

While she changed her clothes and gathered her surfing gear from her closet, Cindy's thoughts had been racing. On the one hand she had to admit that her feelings for Grant had become more than friendly. Especially when he had held her hand. Cindy had looked at her hand. It looked the same. But it felt different. Cindy got a funny feeling in the pit of her stomach. She knew that if she had driven home with Grant, he might have held her hand again. Or even kissed her. And she would have liked that. Very much.

Except her sisters would have been watching. In fact, the whole town might as well have been watching. Overnight Cindy had become some crazy kind of celebrity, and she hated it. Just when she needed some privacy and to have a real heart-to-heart talk with a friend about guys, she couldn't trust that anything she said—even at home— wouldn't get broadcast around the school. Mollie was a one-girl gossip column, and Cindy had a funny feeling that if it hadn't been for Mollie latching on to the idea of her and Grant as a twosome, this whole meet wouldn't have blown into such a big deal. For a little sister she sure had a big mouth.

The walk to the beach had more or less cleared her head. Grant was an opponent until Friday. There was no changing that, but she didn't always have to act so angry with him. In fact, she was beginning to suspect that she got angry with him because she liked him. It made no sense. She didn't understand her feelings. But as she walked down the hill toward the marina, she knew exactly who she had to confide in about the scene at Lookout Point with Grant. Nicole was supposed to be there shooting some pictures for the yearbook.

She'd grab Nicole and drag her out for a Coke and have a real heart-to-heart. Somewhere where Mollie couldn't eavesdrop.

But just at the moment when Cindy realized that she might be falling in love with Grant Mac-Phearson, she had looked down toward the water and seen him holding Nicole in his arms. Nicole, with seaweed wrapped around her ankle, looked like some romantic victim of a shipwreck. They were both laughing, and Grant looked so happy.

Cindy had stood open-mouthed a few yards down the beach, watching them. Her heart had stopped for a minute. When it started up again it hurt in a way it had never hurt her before. Not even the time when she was six years old and had operated on Nicole's favorite teddy bear, tearing it to shreds in the process. Nicole had walked into Cindy's room and started crying and she had told her she was the ugliest, nastiest, meanest sister in the whole wide world.

Chapter 10

*"C*indy, are you feeling all right? You haven't touched your soufflé." Mrs. Lewis glanced across the dinner table at her daughter.

Nicole coughed politely. "I wouldn't say she hasn't touched it." She stared pointedly at Cindy's plate and at Winston, who was resting his huge head on Cindy's knee. Half of Cindy's soufflé had already vanished down the dog's throat.

"Hey, Skipper," Mr. Lewis said, addressing Cindy by his pet name for her. "You know the rules. No feeding animals at the table."

"Winston's not an animal. He's family. Besides, he's not at the table; he's on the floor. His head is on my lap. And I'm not sure I'd call this stuff food!" Cindy snapped, and glared at Nicole. She shoved her plate away, and folded her arms across her chest. "I'd rather have a cheeseburger."

"I think Nicole's soufflé is *extraordinaire;* that's how you say it, isn't it, Nicole?" Mollie asked cheerily. "The perfect topping to an extraordinary day—*un jour extraordinaire.*"

"Let's not go into that again!" Cindy grumbled, and slouched down in her seat.

"Cindy!" her mother exclaimed. "If you're not sick, then mind your manners. Whatever has gotten into you?"

"It's all going to her head. That's what. Oh, Daddy, you should have seen the cafeteria today. Everyone, but *everyone*—of the girls, that is—is supporting Cindy. She's a heroine." Mollie clasped her hands and rolled her eyes.

"What for? Wait. Don't tell me. Let me guess. Cindy broke an all-time school record for detentions doled out in a single week," Mr. Lewis joked. Everyone laughed but Cindy.

"Dad, sometimes you're a bundle of laughs," Cindy said sullenly.

"The surfing competition at the Big Luau," Mollie and Nicole answered at once. Mollie told her father all about the upcoming match. "And it's turned into the sporting event of the decade—"

Cindy interrupted with a scowl. "Tell it like it is. What did the paper call it?—" She paused, "Oh, yes, the Battle of the Sexes." She turned toward her sister. Her voice held a hint of challenge in it as she said, "Isn't that right, Nicole?"

Nicole stopped paring her apple and looked quizzically at her sister. "Yes, that's what they called it in the editorial."

Cindy gave her a cold, accusing look, holding her glance, until Nicole gave a puzzled shrug, looked down, and began slicing the apple in slender sections.

"Don't tell me it's the boys against the girls." Mrs. Lewis gave a tired sigh. "Things never change. It's so silly."

"Oh, I don't think so." Mollie shook her head vehemently. "Not at all. I think it's fun. Especially when the boy in question is the Incredible Hunk himself—Grant MacPhearson."

Cindy went pale. "Can I be excused?"

"Your turn for dishes, isn't it?" Mrs. Lewis reminded her. Cindy began to protest, but her mother silenced her with a hard look. "All this competition with boys, Mollie, is not right in high school," Mrs. Lewis said firmly.

Cindy pursed her lips.

"Hold it, Laura. I disagree," Mr. Lewis broke in. "I think it's great for girls to compete against boys in sports. Girls are just as good as boys in most sports; they just don't have a chance to prove it. Any boy who thinks Cindy's not as good as he is deserves to lose. I'm sure Cindy has a good chance at winning, and I'll be there rooting for her."

"Richard, dear, proving who's stronger or better doesn't make for very good relationships between men and women, does it?"

Mr. Lewis threw his hands up in the air and shrugged his shoulders. "Who's talking about relationships? I thought we were talking about surfing."

Nicole and her mother exchanged a knowing smile. "Men!" they both said at once.

Mr. Lewis turned back to Cindy. "So, Skipper, when is this Big Luau?" he said, pulling a small appointment book out of his jacket pocket.

Cindy stabbed at her placemat with a spoon and mumbled, "You know, Dad, it's really not such a big deal."

"Daddy, don't listen to her. She's just in a weird mood," Mollie said, then playfully waggled her finger in her father's face and scolded, "You haven't been listening. I told you when we sat down for dinner. It's Friday night. And I'm going to go." She jumped up and stood behind his chair and wrapped her arms around his neck. "And I'm going to stay to the bitter end. The party is going to go on and on way past my curfew, but wild horses couldn't keep me away."

"But I can!" her mother warned.

"Oh, Laura, I don't think staying out late just this once will hurt Mollie. Besides, she is in high school now. And her sisters will be there."

Mollie gave a delighted shriek and began clearing the table before her father could change his mind.

"Which Friday?" Mr. Lewis asked, pushing his chair back from the table.

"This week, Dad," Nicole replied. "The contest will be around five. The party afterward."

"This week!" Mr. Lewis roared. "It can't be. I've got tickets."

"Calm down, Richard. I'm sure we can give them away. The Roswells always like to take in a show."

"Give them away?" Mr. Lewis stammered incredulously. "Do you have any idea what I went through to get them? I begged, borrowed, and stole to get these two tickets for the Dodgers/Mets game at the stadium. Cindy and I are going to that game and that's that."

"But the contest! The Luau. Grant!" Mollie wailed, poking her head back into the room.

"Hold it!" Cindy suddenly sprang up. Her face was pale and her lips were trembling. "Dad, if you had bothered to tell me you were trying to get the tickets I could have spared you all that trouble. I don't care if you have tickets for the first passenger ship to the moon. I can't back down from this contest against that creep MacPhearson." Cindy paused and looked nastily at a bewildered Nicole. She turned back to her father and continued, her voice rising with every word, "You didn't even ask me if I wanted to go. You just took it for granted. Cindy's loved going to ball games since she was seven years old. But I'm not seven anymore. Or hasn't anyone noticed? No girl my age goes to ball games with her dad. You can keep your tickets." She shot another hostile look at Nicole, then added cryptically, "Of course, going to a ball game would be the perfect excuse for skipping the luau. Nicole *and* Grant would be the two happiest people in the world if I didn't show up Friday night. Right?" she asked spitefully, then bounded out of the room and up the stairs two at a time, loudly slamming the door to her room.

Mollie whistled from the kitchen. "Nicole, why is she so mad at you?"

Nicole shrugged, slowly shook her head, and looked up the stairs.

Mr. Lewis sat dumbfounded, looking up toward Cindy's room. "I thought she really would love to go to the game. How could I know about this Big Luau? After all, it's the first game of the National League Playoffs—" His voice trailed off.

"Richard, let me go and talk to her. Something's really bothering her. Cindy never acts this way." Mrs. Lewis patted her husband's shoulder; then she started for the stairs.

"Non, Maman, let me," Nicole said quietly. "I have an idea what this might be about." She gestured toward the kitchen. "Keep Mollie out of this, *please.*" With that Nicole headed up the steps.

Nicole rapped gently on Cindy's door. "Cindy, open up. Come on. You can't stay locked in your room forever." Nicole pressed her ear to the door. Not a sound. She debated with herself an instant, then knocked again. "Cindy, if you don't come out now and talk to me, I'm going to get Mom." She waited to let the words sink in. "And I think I'm the person you really want to talk to, right?"

Nicole closed her eyes, held her breath, and kept her ear to the door. A second later she opened them and breathed a sigh of relief. A second after that Cindy flung open the door.

"Cindy, you've been crying!" Nicole instantly tried to put her hand on her sister's shoulder.

But Cindy, recoiling from Nicole's touch, gave a short, cynical laugh. "Oh, I keep forgetting; I'm the Lewis sister who's not supposed to cry." She rubbed her sleeve against her nose and stared coldly at Nicole.

Cindy looked so hurt and angry. Nicole frowned and shook her head. "I don't understand. What's going on? Are you going to let me in so we can talk about it—whatever it is?" Nicole asked.

Cindy closed her eyes and leaned her head back against the doorframe. After a moment's hesitation, she walked back into her room without saying a word and threw herself facedown on the bed. Nicole followed, quietly shutting the door behind her. Moving a tennis racket off the chair, she sat down and waited for Cindy to speak.

But Cindy couldn't speak; she just sat there looking so miserable that Nicole, sounding scared, said, "Cindy. What happened?"

Suddenly Cindy sat bolt upright on the bed, hugged her pillow to her chest, and looked accusingly at Nicole. She stammered, "How could you, Nicole? How could you do it? And then to pretend you don't know what's going on?"

Nicole's frightened expression gave way to a puzzled frown. "Cindy, please, I really don't know what you're talking about. What did I do?"

Cindy threw her pillow angrily across the floor and leaped to her feet. She yanked some tissues out of the box on her night table and began shredding them as she spoke. "How can you sit there, calmly denying it? Denying you stole Grant right out from under my nose—"

"Stole Grant?" Nicole repeated incredulously. "Whatever are you talking about?"

"I saw you. I saw both of you. The whole thing today down on the beach. The way he was holding you, the way he looked—" Cindy, with tears in her eyes, flopped back down on her bed.

"Oh, no!" Nicole cried. "Cindy, you've got it all wrong."

Cindy looked up. "Stop it, Nicole. You sound like a dumb soap opera."

"I do not," Nicole said firmly. "Because you *do* have it all wrong, you idiot. I can't believe you would think—even for a minute—I'd steal a guy from anyone, let alone my own sister." Nicole's face was flushed, her eyes steely. Then she looked at her tear-stained sister, her expression softened, and she sat down on the bed next to her. "All I did was walk up to Grant to talk to him about the Big Luau." Nicole hesitated, then squeezed her eyes shut, and admitted, "I was going to try to talk him out of the whole thing—to give you two a chance."

Cindy snorted scornfully.

"I was!" Nicole declared, then told Cindy about Grant's outburst. "I got so angry I stormed off and tripped in the seaweed and he saved me."

"He saved you?" Cindy repeated skeptically.

Nicole nodded. "Well, he caught me, and then I realized he really is a nice guy—who likes you very much, Cindy. And I also saw that I was right all along. He's just upset because he thinks you only want to compete with him. I think he wants you to surf *with* him, not *against* him."

Cindy looked directly at Nicole and searched her eyes. Nicole was telling the truth. Part of Cindy was relieved; the rest of her felt utterly, hopelessly miserable. "Oh, Nicole, I really blew it. If you only knew what happened today." She told Nicole about her encounter with Grant on Lookout Point.

Nicole stared incredulously at her sister, and then shook her head in disgust. "You are the most impossible girl who ever existed when it comes to guys. You couldn't do more things wrong if you tried, Cindy. Honestly, I think you should start reading the advice-to-the-lovelorn column in Mollie's *Seventeen*s. Otherwise, you're never going to get a guy."

Cindy jumped up from the bed and began to pace the floor. "Here we go again!" she shouted.

"How many times do I have to tell you I don't want to 'get a guy.'"

Nicole grinned. Cindy was back in her old form. "No, that's right. You don't want to get a guy, you want to lose him!"

"I do not!" Cindy sputtered, her red-rimmed eyes flashing. She repeated earnestly, "No, I don't want to lose him." She shot a pleading glance at her sister. "Oh, Nicole, what should I do?" she wailed, leaning against the dresser and propping her chin in her hands. "Have I blown it?" she asked, afraid to hear Nicole's answer.

Nicole took a deep breath. "I—I don't know, Cindy. I really don't know if you've blown it. But my feeling is, Grant really likes you and—" She paused, gritted her teeth, and met Cindy's worried glance. "You're not going to like this," Nicole warned.

Cindy sat down meekly next to Nicole on the bed. "What? What should I do?" she asked in a small voice. "I really like him, Nicole. Oh, I do!" she suddenly confided, and blushed and quickly turned her face away from her sister.

"Drop out of the meet."

Cindy shook her head slowly. "Oh, Nicole. How can I do a thing like that now? Too much is at stake."

Nicole was adamant. "You've got the perfect excuse—the Dodgers/Yankee game—"

"Dodgers/Mets; it's not the World Series yet," Cindy corrected.

"*C'est la même chose.* It's the same thing," Nicole declared with an impatient wave of her hand. "The game's not the point, but it's the one way to bow out gracefully."

"But it's not just my match against Grant anymore. The whole school's involved. You know that. Backing down now," Cindy started, "it's impossible. So many kids are depending on me to win."

"I know how important winning is to you." Nicole grabbed her sister's hand. "But winning isn't everything in life—especially if it leaves you lonely."

Cindy kicked her feet disconsolately against the bed. She looked around her room. Trophies and prizes cluttered the desk, the dresser, the windowsills, and half the shelves. Blue ribbons hung from the brightly postered walls. Her heart caught in her throat as she looked at the Vista High pennant tacked above her mirror. She had always been a winner, a keen competitor, and a real champion for her school. If she gave up now, how would she ever face her crowd again? She shook her head, then thought of Grant. Was he worth it? She pressed her palms to her forehead and squeezed her eyes shut and instantly remembered how warm Grant's hand had felt when she had held it briefly that afternoon. Yes, he was worth it.

With a defeated sigh she looked directly at Nicole. "Okay. You win. I'll talk to him tomorrow at school. Maybe he can help me find a way out of this—gracefully—as you like to put it," Cindy said flatly. She was doing the right thing. She was almost sure of that. Except it felt so absolutely, completely, totally wrong.

Winston suddenly began barking furiously; then the doorbell rang. "Who's that?" Nicole asked.

"Beats me." Cindy shrugged and toyed with the fringe on her old blue bedspread. A familiar deep voice drifted up the stairs. Cindy's eyes opened wide. She grabbed her sister's arm. "Nicole, it's Grant!"

"What's he doing here?" Nicole gasped. Cindy shook her head.

"Cindy," their mother's voice called up the stairs. "A young man's here to see you. Can you come down?"

Before Cindy could answer, footsteps clattered up the stairs, the door to her room burst open, and Mollie flew in. "It's him," she squealed. "Grant. He's here. He wants you to go out with him. Oh, Cindy, I'm going to faint!" Mollie promptly collapsed gracefully on the bed.

"Cindy?" their mother called again.

"She's coming, Mom," Nicole yelled down.

Mollie's head popped up. She stared at Cindy critically and made a face. "Ugh, you look awful." Her expression softened. "Hey, Cin—you've been crying. What's going on here?" she whispered.

Cindy started to say something, but Nicole broke in. "Nothing, Mollie. Nothing at all. Cindy's fine.

Why don't you go to your room and find her some of that perfume you bought last week and let her get ready to see Grant. Okay?" Nicole took Mollie by the shoulders and shoved her out the door, closing it firmly behind her.

"That'll keep her safely out of the way for a while—and away from Grant!" Nicole declared, and threw open Cindy's closet.

"I can't see him looking like this!" Cindy looked in the mirror and tried to rub the red out of her eyes with her fist.

"Let your big sister take care of you for a change."

Cindy gritted her teeth but submitted.

Five minutes later, Cindy stood in front of the mirror, awkwardly surveying her reflection. "Ugh, this makeup feels funny."

"I know. And you don't usually need it, but it helps when you're blotchy from crying. Doesn't it?"

"Yeah, I guess you're the expert in that department." Cindy laughed nervously.

Cindy did look more put together. She had on her skirt and a turquoise-blue tank top and Nicole's new white windbreaker. Nicole had done something very subtle with eye makeup so Cindy's eyes didn't look as red anymore. She wriggled her toes in the white sandals she had borrowed from her sister. "Gosh, I couldn't walk far in these."

"He has a car, doesn't he?" Nicole said wryly.

"So you won't have to walk far, and if you go to the beach, take them off."

Just then Mollie burst back into the room and announced breathlessly, "Here it is—*Je reviens*. Isn't that romantic? And it smells so—"

Cindy wrinkled her nose. "No, that's too much. I can't wear it. Oh, please, Nicole." She backed off from her sister as Nicole went to dab some of Mollie's perfume behind Cindy's ears.

"There, just a little. And now you're off." She began pushing Cindy toward the door.

Mollie clapped her hands. "You look so pretty, Cindy."

Cindy gave an embarrassed grin. "I do?"

Nicole nodded. "You do—and remember, this is your big chance. To talk to Grant. Like we decided just now, right?" Nicole held Cindy's arm a minute.

Cindy closed her eyes, took a deep breath, and gulped. "Right," she whispered, then repeated it loud and clear as Nicole marched her out of the bedroom door. "Right!" But deep down inside the idea of dropping out still felt all wrong.

Chapter 11

*B*y the time Grant and Cindy got to the beach she decided she really might be falling in love with him. Winston obviously adored him.

Cindy hadn't planned on taking Winston with them for a walk. But when she came downstairs and Grant asked if she preferred a ride down to Taco Rio or a walk on the beach, her father, peering sternly over his paper, had commented in his don't-give-me-an-argument-about-it voice that Winston was in dire need of exercise. Normally, Cindy would have argued the point, but her father was still edgy over the scene at the dinner table, and Cindy hadn't had time to apologize yet. She knew better than to push her luck. And she suddenly felt sorry for her dad. In the space of a couple of hours, the one daughter he could count on to be sensible and not boy-crazy had turned down tickets to an important baseball game and was walking out the door with a tall, handsome stranger on her first date.

Even in her wildest dreams, however, Cindy had never pictured her first date including Winston. And neither had her sisters nor her mother, who all gathered at the study window to watch Cindy, Grant, and Winston primly head down the driveway, past the red Trans Am, out onto Hacienda Road, and down the hill toward the shore.

Unfortunately, Grant didn't say or do anything en route to the beach to make Cindy feel more comfortable. In fact, outside of a few semistuttered remarks—"Uh, it's nice around here" and "Umm, the moon's almost full. It's so bright out you don't need a flashlight"—Grant said absolutely nothing. Maybe having a boyfriend meant not saying very much, Cindy thought, not sure what she felt about keeping quiet so long. Not that it mattered at the moment. She was too nervous to say anything herself. Besides, she kept thinking how nice it would be to hold Grant's hand, and the thought made her blush. But her hands seemed to have a will of their own. She kept wanting to touch his shoulder or take his arm, so to avoid doing anything embarrassing, she turned up the collar of her jacket and stuffed her fists into her pockets. The whole way to the beach she walked a good two feet apart from him.

They picked their way carefully along the kelp-strewn sand, heading toward the water. The tide was high, and the surf was rough and pounding. The moonlight was bright enough to see the shape of things: driftwood washed up since the afternoon, the ghostly outline of the park service trash cans, the aluminum sides of the locked-up Snack Shack. The squeak of the boats rocking in their berths in the marina drifted toward them on the wind. Cindy noticed a couple of cars in the far corner of the lot and grinned. She started to make a crazy remark about kids parking, then remembered that she was on a date with Grant, not walking with Duffy or her friends.

She was still feeling embarrassed about almost sticking her foot in her mouth, when Grant finally spoke. He was playing fetch with Winston by tossing a stick into the waves. All of a sudden, he said quietly, "I thought we should be alone. Because I want to talk to you."

Cindy nodded. "I guess we're on the same wavelength." She laughed nervously. "I wanted to talk to you, too—alone."

Neither said anything for a second, until finally Grant spoke up. "You know, from the first time I saw you, I really liked you. I wanted to be your friend. I still do." His words came in spurts. Cindy suddenly wanted to hug him, to say everything's okay. But she didn't know if she could. Meanwhile he continued, "About the meet and all. I'm really sorry about the whole mess." Cindy glanced up at him. He looked so handsome standing there in the moonlight, gazing out to sea as he spoke. Cindy sighed and started to speak.

"It's gone beyond the point of mess," she said, kicking a clump of seaweed with her foot.

He laughed and looked down at her. For a second she thought he was going to kiss her, but instead he cleared his throat and tugged the stick away from Winston and tossed it further down the beach. "But even if you hadn't met the challenge, I would have liked you anyway. Really I would," he said earnestly. "You're a really great girl, and one of the best surfers I've ever seen—"

Cindy couldn't resist. "Even in Hawaii?"

Grant chuckled. "Even in Hawaii." Then he added hesitantly, "So that's why I don't want you to go through with this."

"You mean you want me to drop out?" Cindy gasped, afraid to believe her ears.

"Right. I mean this whole stupid business of pretending to drown and throwing the race so I can win, just because you feel the same way about me that I feel about you, is kind of silly." Grant spoke quickly. "And you're too good an athlete to do that. Besides, you might get hurt."

Cindy had stopped kicking the seaweed. For a second, she stopped breathing. "Wait," she said slowly, "let me see if I heard you right. You think that because I like you—because you *think* I like you—I'm going to pull a rotten, sneaky, lowdown trick like that?" Cindy's voice rose. "That's the craziest idea I've ever heard," she cried. But even as she spoke she knew that she had heard it all before. She'd kill Mollie when she got home, if she didn't die of embarrassment first.

"Oh, Cindy, don't try to deny it. It's all over town," Grant groaned. "I mean, that's why I wanted to talk to you before school tomorrow. You're going to look like a fool. I just thought we could settle all this between ourselves and I could help you save face and all that."

"Save face!" Cindy repeated scornfully. "A fool? You are—you are incredible, Grant. How could you believe that I'd do that?"

In the heat of the moment Cindy forgot that there *was* a reason why he'd think she'd pull such a silly stunt. "If you think you can sweet-talk me out of this race, you've got another think coming," Cindy fumed, and stomped up and down, a confused Winston at her heels. "I've heard of ego before," she roared, "but you've got the biggest, most inflated macho ego in the history of the world, that's what you have, Grant MacPhearson, and you'd better just watch out. Come Friday, you're going to get yours."

"I'm going to get mine!" Grant yelled, and slapped his hand against his forehead and raised his eyes toward heaven. "Help me," he implored. Then he turned to Cindy. "You're just as bad. In fact, you're worse than most of them. You go around blaming everything on the male ego. Well, Cindy Lewis, before you start talking about my ego, take a good look at yourself sometime. You've got it coming to you Friday. You want a battle, you're getting an all-out war, and you"—Grant tapped her on the shoulder with his finger—"you are going to lose. You're going to see some surfing you'll never forget."

Grant stomped back toward the parking lot, yelling over his shoulder, "And when you pretend to drown, don't expect me to save you!"

With an angry toss of her head, Cindy whirled around and stormed back up the beach. After only a few steps, she remembered that Grant's car was still in her driveway. "Oh, Winston, what'll I do?" she wailed, and stood forlornly on the sand. She had never felt so angry, humiliated, and hurt in her whole life. "If I go home now, I'd run into him, and I never ever want to see him again." She stomped her foot and crossed her arms across her chest and looked around. The marina dock was still all lit up, and some people were having a party on one of the boats. After a minute she headed over there. The snack bar would still be open. She'd buy a Coke. That would give Grant enough time to get his car and be long gone before she went home.

As she neared the pier, the sound of a Beach Boys tune floated out over the water. Cindy stared a minute at the bright lights and changed her mind about the Coke. She needed to be alone. She had to rethink things fast. Winning Friday was more important than ever. If she lost, no one would ever believe that she hadn't lost on purpose. She sat down on the dock and dangled her legs over the water. How had she ever gotten in such a mess to begin with?

Winston flopped down beside her, resting his head in her lap. "Winston," she lamented, "men!" Winston gave an indignant woof. Cindy affectionately tugged his ears. "Not you, silly. You can't help being a boy dog." Then she buried her face in his thick, soft fur and for the second time that night started to cry.

Chapter 12

*G*rant's car was gone when she finally returned home. And the walk had only given her time to grow more furious with Mollie. Storming in the front door, she started past her father's study. He looked up from his drawing table and flashed her a warm smile. "Cindy," he said happily, "Nicole told me you changed your mind and are coming with me to the game."

"Nicole did what!" she cried. She was so furious at Grant and Mollie, she had momentarily forgotten her earlier decision to quit the competition. She took a swift, deep breath. "I don't believe this. I really don't believe this!" She threw her arms up in the air. "No way, Dad—oh, just forget it," she sputtered, and ran up the stairs.

"Cindy," he called after her, "what's going on around here?" But Cindy didn't answer; she was already in Mollie's room.

Mollie and Nicole sat cross-legged together on the bed. Ten bottles of nail polish were lined up on the cluttered night table. Nicole was almost finished painting Mollie's fingernails—each one a different color. When Cindy marched in, Mollie had her head thrown back and her eyes squeezed shut, as if she were trying to remember something.

"I know." Mollie opened her eyes and her face lit up as she began conjugating a French verb. *J'aime, tu aimes—*"

"You're dead, Mollie Lewis." Cindy stood in the doorway.

"What? What are you doing back so soon?" Mollie asked, looking past Cindy's shoulder, half expecting to see Grant.

"Oh, boy!" Nicole muttered under her breath. Aloud she said, "Something went wrong—didn't it?—with our plan."

Cindy dismissed Nicole and the plan with an impatient wave of her hand. She didn't take her eyes off Mollie's face. "Anything that could possibly go wrong did!" she exclaimed, and told them about her encounter on the beach.

She walked into the messy room and tossed a pile of clothes off a chair onto the floor. She turned the chair around, straddled it, and looked Mollie directly in the eye. "Now, where do you think Grant got that idea of me throwing the race—by pretending to drown?"

Mollie's big blue eyes widened innocently. "How would I know? I certainly never mentioned it!"

Nicole dipped the brush back into the nail polish and slowly began painting Mollie's pinkie green. "Mollie," she said quietly, "you *have* been talking about Grant and Cindy nonstop for almost a week now!"

"So? So have you. So has Cindy. Everyone has! In fact, today after school everyone was talking about Grant and Cindy at the Taco Rio. You'd be real proud of me, Cin. That weird Margie Waxman suggested that since Grant was acting like he had a crush on you—"

"Some crush!" Cindy scoffed.

Mollie continued without missing a beat, "—he would probably throw the race to be absolutely sure you'd win. You should have heard me. I told Margie, in no uncertain terms, that throwing a race was too unsportsmanlike for a guy like Grant. That's the word you used the other day, isn't it—unsportsmanlike?"

Cindy leaned forward against the back of the chair. Her eyes narrowed as she regarded her sister. "What else did you say?" she asked in a deliberate, slow voice.

"I told them you'd never throw a race either. Even though," Mollie giggled sheepishly, "I said you were crazy not to."

"You what?" Nicole gasped. "Oh, Mollie, when will you learn to keep your mouth shut!"

"Wait, wait. Let me finish my story." Mollie pouted. "I said that Cindy was crazy and that in her shoes—or on her surfboard—I'd make sure I'd be in a situation where Grant would have to rescue me." The words were barely out when Mollie clapped her wet nail-polished hand to her mouth. "Oh, no!" she shrieked. "I bet people overheard me say that. The place was so crowded. They must have thought I meant you were planning to be rescued. People must have gotten the wrong idea. Someone must have told Grant. Oh, Cindy, I could just die."

"I knew it!" Cindy jumped up. "Of all the possible kid sisters in the world, I had to get stuck with you," she fumed. "What's between Grant and me is my business, not yours, and certainly not half of Santa Barbara's!"

Two big tears started down from Mollie's eyes. "I—I didn't mean to make trouble. Really I didn't." She sniffed and turned to Nicole for support. Nicole just shook her head.

"Mollie, you couldn't have made things worse if you tried." Then Nicole turned to Cindy and said calmly, "But Cindy, it's not so bad. Now that you are going to drop out of the competition, none of this matters."

"Drop out!" Mollie was flabbergasted. "But she can't—the whole school . . ." she blubbered.

"Right, Mollie, the whole school. And I expect

by tomorrow, the whole school—thanks to you—will hear that I *thought* of dropping out, except I'm not dropping out," Cindy declared fiercely. "Far from it."

"But you promised." Nicole's hands went limp in her lap. Cindy's face was set in a familiar, obstinate expression. Nothing, not even an earthquake, would budge her now.

"Right. Before Grant told me all about that cute little rumor started by our sister here." She cast Mollie a scornful look and stood up. "So, Mollie, you'll get your competition. And Grant's going to get what's coming to him."

"Oh, Cindy, please think about it. Don't make any decisions until morning. You'll see things more clearly then," Nicole reasoned.

"Sometimes I think you live on another planet. Don't you see? If I drop out, or if I stay in and happen to lose, people will say I'm trying to make Grant look good because I want him to be my boyfriend. And that's absolutely the last thing I want people to think. So there's no decision to make." Cindy gave Mollie one last devastating look, and flounced out the door.

From outside her own room she called back over her shoulder, "I'm staying in the competition, and I'm going to win. No one or nothing can stop me now!"

Chapter 13

*C*indy stood on the outskirts of the crowd already gathered on the beach for the Big Luau. Beneath her wet suit she was wearing her lucky blue-and-green striped racing tank: the same bathing suit she had worn the summer before when she won the California State Junior Surfing Title at Redondo Beach. A stiff breeze blew in from the water, ruffling Cindy's hair. She looked calm, strong, and confident enough to conquer any wave, but as she eyed the choppy sea, she was shaking like a leaf inside. Cindy had never felt so scared and lonely in her whole life.

She looked over toward the already blazing bonfire near what seemed to be some invisible boundary line drawn between the guys and the girls. Cindy bit her lip, then tossed her head proudly and looked away. Duffy was there in the thick of things, horsing around with Joey, Matt Darcy, and Brett Harrington. Grant was with them, wearing his wet suit and leaning against his bright orange surfboard, laughing and joking and acting as if this were a normal Friday-afternoon bash on the beach—not fifteen minutes before zero hour and the battle of the sexes. He looked very cute, very confident, and not at all like her worst enemy in the whole wide world.

Cindy turned away from the boisterous scene and walked slowly down the beach away from all the kids. Watching Grant made her stomach churn, and watching the other guys—especially Duffy— hurt too much. Sure, Duffy had waved to her when she came down the beach, but he hadn't walked up to her or wished her luck or told one of his dumb surfing jokes. He had stayed with the other guys and Grant. Cindy realized that she hadn't said more than three words to Duffy for almost a whole week.

That afternoon Cindy had hung out with Anna and the other girls until the pom-pom squad turned up wearing yellow Vista High sweat shirts and carrying homemade "Cindy is our Numero Uno!" banners. Cindy had suddenly felt really dumb and embarrassed and mumbled something about needing some quiet to concentrate on her game plan. The girls looked disappointed, but didn't protest when Cindy marched off, with her surfboard under her arm, to a more deserted stretch of beach near the lagoon.

But she really had no game plan. In fact, as she sat down on the sand and propped her chin in her hands, she wasn't really thinking about the competition at all. She was thinking about Grant, and what she *should* be feeling at that moment: an overwhelming desire to win. What she *was* feeling, however, was an overwhelming desire to be with Grant—to talk to him, to watch him smile, to walk somewhere away from all these people on the beach, to get to know him better, to hold his hand, to kiss him. Just a few minutes before her "battle" against Grant was due to begin, Cindy knew that in spite of what she had told her friends, her sisters, and herself, she didn't hate Grant MacPhearson at all. She loved him.

And loving Grant was crazy, because after today, they'd probably never talk to each other again.

"There she is!" Mollie cried as she and Nicole approached Cindy. The two girls were trudging down the beach, carrying a couple of beach towels and a small cooler. Nicole was swathed from head to toe in white gauzy pants, a long-sleeved shirt, and her new straw hat. Mollie was wearing her bikini and struggling not to look too pleased at the chorus of whistles that followed her progress down the boys' side of the beach.

Mollie reached Cindy first. She smiled tentatively and waved her fingers in her sister's face.

"Get lost!" Cindy growled. She hadn't spoken to Mollie since Wednesday night.

Mollie looked hurt, but flopped down on the blanket anyway. Nicole dropped down beside her and smiled at Cindy.

"At least you didn't get detention today. Too bad we didn't think of that one to get you out of this race," she said lightheartedly. Cindy gave her a dirty look, and Nicole added quickly, "Not that there's any question of that now. And in case you care, we're both rooting for you."

"Rah, rah!" Cindy snorted, then added, "And don't forget I already had detention yesterday, so, unlike my competition, I couldn't even get down here to practice."

Mollie shook her head. "You know, sometimes you make no sense. If I were in a meet like this, I wouldn't do something so dumb the day before."

"We all know what you would do, Mollie, if you were in a meet like this!" Cindy said sharply. Actually yesterday's detention was pretty silly. The sight of all the boys hanging out together in the hall, hassling all the girls who walked by, had finally driven her crazy, and she had felt like making some trouble for the boys. So she had commandeered a squad of girls from the water polo and swim teams and sneaked into the boys' locker room at lunch. They were in the middle of spraying the mirrors with shaving cream when the security guard caught them. Cindy stepped forward as ringleader and had yet one more memorable interview with the principal. The result was detention, causing her to miss her last chance to work out before the contest.

Cindy pointedly looked away from her sisters and out over the lagoon. She wished they would leave her alone.

Nicole cleared her throat and said quietly, "You know, this bad mood isn't going to help a thing. You're wasting a lot of energy being nasty to Mollie. You'd be better off directing your anger toward winning today."

"Now you want me to win!" Cindy said caustically, and angrily tossed some pebbles across the water. They landed halfway across the lagoon.

Suddenly Mollie jumped up and planted her hands on her hips. She stared down at her sister and shook her head in disgust. "You know, Cindy, I don't care if you win or lose anymore. In fact, no one does. You're acting like such a creep—like a born loser. Looking at you now, I can't believe you've ever won a thing in your life," Mollie sneered.

"What!" Cindy exclaimed. One look at Mollie's flushed, angry face convinced Cindy that Mollie wasn't kidding. "You don't know what you're talking about." Cindy waved Mollie off, but her voice had a defensive edge to it.

"Yes, she does!" Nicole declared. "In fact, you're supposed to be one of the co-stars in this dumb contest, but I bet you haven't been on your surfboard since the weekend, right?"

Cindy didn't reply. She dug her toes into the sand while Nicole continued. "You look exactly like pictures I've seen of someone who's already lost a big race. And it hasn't even started yet. Look at yourself, Cindy." Nicole shook her sister's arm. "If you really believe what you've been saying all week—that the girls of Vista are counting on you—you'd better pull yourself together. I'm getting sick of looking at the guys on one side and the girls on the other. I think everyone's getting sick of it. And you're supposed to be the girl who can save the day. I still think it's all ridiculous, but there's no changing things now, so you'd just better forget about whatever's bothering you and concentrate on the match. You've got"—Nicole checked her watch—"exactly ten minutes to begin to look like a winner."

Cindy inhaled deeply and looked back toward the crowd. She tried not to single out Grant, but it was impossible. She shook her head and cupped her chin in her hands. "I can't . . . I can't concentrate on the match," she said in a flat, defeated voice.

Mollie dropped down next to Cindy and winked at Nicole. "Sure you can. Remember what you told me about visualizing doing something well, then doing it for real and always succeeding. Isn't that how you win swim meets? It's simple. Just picture yourself winning." Mollie snapped her fingers. "And presto, you'll win. And then no one can ever say anything bad about you and Grant and throwing the competition again."

Cindy looked up at her sisters in disgust. "I don't believe this. The two of you giving me a rap on sports psychology," she said scornfully, then stood up, and began dusting the sand off her wet suit. "Neither of you knows the first thing about sports." She looked from Nicole to Mollie, and her expression softened slightly. "Oh, I don't know." She kicked at her surfboard. "I guess you're just trying to be helpful. But don't you understand? Besides the fact I feel crummy right now, competing against Grant, I really think he is better than me. I've never seen a better surfer. And so much is at stake." She waved back toward the crowd around the bonfire. Anna stood at the fringe and spotted Cindy. She waved frantically in her direction. Her voice was drowned out by the noise of the surf, but obviously the match was about to start.

"Forget about Grant!" Mollie said suddenly. "Don't think about him at all. Not how you feel about him. Not about how he surfs. Think about surfing. Think about whatever it is you feel when you ride that thing." She pointed to the surfboard. "That's how kids in the Olympics win gold medals. I was reading all about Peggy Fleming and how she used to think before a competition—I can't remember if it was *Young Miss* or *Seventeen* or ..." Mollie's puzzled expression cracked Cindy up. Nicole followed suit.

"Mollie, for once, I'm glad you read *Seventeen.*" Cindy breathed a sigh of relief. "I had forgotten all about that. My head's been screwed on all wrong lately."

"Sophomore slump!" Nicole pronounced, and, jumping up, linked her arm through Cindy's. "But this is not the time to be slumping. Stand tall, little sister. I know you're going to win."

"Me too!" Mollie grinned. "I've always known. And not just the race!" she added wickedly.

"Little sisters," Cindy groaned as Mollie grabbed her other arm. Cindy tried to glare at the irrepressible Mollie, but she couldn't, because Mollie had just given her a brilliant idea. Visualizing winning a race usually worked. Why not visualize winning Grant?

"Imagine having two little sisters!" Nicole sniffed haughtily as the three girls paraded back toward the bonfire arm in arm.

"I can't." Cindy giggled nervously. "I'm too busy imagining winning." To herself she added, "And trying to imagine not losing Grant."

Chapter 14

7he luck of the draw left Cindy last, and she had won her first skirmish in the battle of the sexes. Going last was a matter of principle. Grant had quickly suggested to the judges that it was only right for the girl to go first. The girls' cheering section had burst into a deafening boo, and Cindy had stood up and said, no way. This was a surfing competition, not some old-fashioned parlor game, and she insisted that they draw straws to determine who began the competition.

The judges agreed with her—unanimously. That gave Cindy heart. It wasn't until she saw the three guys and three girls, all seniors, from the various water sports teams, that she realized she had chosen what was sure to be a hung jury. She should have gotten one extra person—maybe the swim coach—to act as tie breaker. Now no one would win the race. The guys would surely give Grant more points. And the girls would favor Cindy.

After all the hoopla that had surrounded the event, a tie would surely be a letdown. Unless, of course, there was no tie. Cindy bit her lip. She thought of Mollie's reaction to Grant ever since she had first laid eyes on the handsome boy. Anna, Carey, and Laura had all felt the same way. Grant was too gorgeous for words. Maybe the girls would vote for Grant because he was cute. Cindy couldn't imagine the boys voting for her— for an instant, she was jealous of her sisters. If only she were pretty and delicate like Nicole, or curvy and cute like Mollie. Instead, she was stuck with being ordinary, blond, and freckled. Her hand strayed to her nose. She wondered if anyone noticed she wasn't wearing her sunblock.

After Kip Evans, the captain of the boys' water polo team, explained the point system for scoring to the spectators, Grant took to the water. The cheers instantly died down, and a hush fell over the crowd.

Cindy was sitting in the front row. She leaned forward and propped her chin on her knees. As she watched Grant paddle out beyond the breakers, something inside her snapped to attention. A smile crossed her face. This always happened just before any competitive event: All her energy would suddenly focus on the competition. All other thoughts, worry, and fears would vanish from her head. She would watch and weigh every movement of her opponent. Now she was watching Grant with the same detachment she had watched the kids at the competition at Redondo Beach last summer.

For the first time, Cindy had a strong, certain feeling that she was going to win. But watching Grant made her realize that winning was really going to be hard. He was a tough competitor—a worthy opponent if she'd ever seen one.

He was out beyond the rough breakers in no time. That should earn him some points before he even got on his surfboard. She shielded her eyes from the low-lying sun and squinted to see him better. He was waiting for the right wave. He almost chose one, hesitated, and then suddenly made his move. Instantly, Cindy knew he had chosen wrong.

But his form was so good that it didn't seem to matter. He glided easily from his knees into a low crouch and was soon standing on his surfboard, gracefully riding the curl in toward the shore. With subtle, swift shifts of his knees and shoulders, he manipulated the board, so that he always stayed just ahead of the breaking wave. Darn, Cindy thought, he makes it look so easy—as if it takes no strength—but she knew that it took a lot of strength. And with high tide, a full moon, and another storm brewing somewhere out beyond the horizon a day or two away in the middle of the Pacific, she knew how rough the water was.

By the time Grant touched down in the swirling foam, several yards down the beach from the crowd, everyone—boys and girls alike—had jumped to their feet. There was no question that he had done a great job. Cindy's work was cut out for her.

Then the scores went up. First the boys held up their scorecards. Grant had scored, on a ten-point basis, two eights and one nine. A groan went up from the girls' side of the beach. Then the girl judges held up their cards. Cindy gasped in horror. One seven and two nines. The total was 8.33. That was as high as Cindy's score in last summer's statewide competition.

"They scored him high because he's cute!" Mollie complained, glaring at the girl judges.

"I'm sure of it!" Carey burst in. Nicole swiftly agreed, though she still hadn't figured out exactly what the scores were based on.

"No," Cindy said firmly. "That's not true. I would have scored him the same way. Maybe even higher." She heaved a sigh, bent down, picked up her surfboard, and started off toward the shoreline. "Wish me luck," she murmured to her sisters as she walked by. But her request was drowned out by the cheers led by the pom-pom girls.

But Cindy wasn't listening to the cheers. Her mind was on the waves. She counted as she walked into the water. Every fourth wave in a group of waves seemed to be the largest. That was it. That was the advantage she could have over Grant. He hadn't waited out the biggest wave. He had been in a rush, but a surfer's ace in the hole was waiting. She would force herself to be patient and then ride a bigger, more dramatic wave in. If she didn't wipe out, she might still win the competition, even if the boys were tempted to score her low, and even if Grant really was the stronger surfer.

Once beyond the breakers, she clung to her surfboard, looking out to sea. She rested a few minutes, counting the sets of waves again. She had been right. She just had to wait for the fourth wave. She forced herself to relax, took five slow, deep breaths, closed her eyes briefly, and pictured exactly how she'd look riding her board in. Her body could feel every movement of the waves underneath her and their rhythm. So, when the right wave came, Cindy was prepared.

Her timing was perfect. She was up from her crouch in no time. For a minute the surfboard vibrated like crazy in the choppy water, but Cindy knew she was in control. And knowing that, Cindy felt like a bird suddenly set free. There was no more war between herself and Grant. There was nothing to prove; there was just herself and the water. And she knew in her heart that Grant had felt the same way a few minutes ago. As soon as she touched down she would find him and tell him that it didn't matter who had won or lost.

And they could talk together about how great the feeling was of being part of the wild frenzied dance of the surf.

She smiled gleefully as she angled the board along the side of the wave. Easily shifting her weight, first to the right, then to the left, she moved her arms out to help her balance. The salty spray stung her face; her legs ached, and the low sun dancing on the water hurt her eyes, but the feeling was like flying, and it was the best feeling in the world.

As she neared the shore, she kicked out into the whirling foam and started shouting and shaking her fists up in the air. She touched down easily, giving a big loud whoop. Everyone thought she was cheering because she felt she had won. But Cindy was yelling because she had just hitched a ride on a great wave, and she felt like singing, and since she couldn't carry a tune, shouting would have to do. Anyway, to Cindy, the ocean felt more like an all-out whoop and shout than like a song.

The six cheerleaders and Anna, Carey, and Mollie were the first to reach her as she lugged her board out of the water and onto the sand. Suddenly the whole world seemed to be hugging her at once. She knocked the water out of her ear, while Anna shouldered her surfboard. The crowd escorted her back down the beach in front of the judges' stand where Nicole was helping her peel off her wet suit, when the scores went up.

Cindy squinted. The boys' scores: 8, 8.5, 9. The girls: 9, 9, 8.5. She heard the screams and shouts first, then she heard herself screaming. "I won! I won!" It was only by three-tenths of a point, but it was enough—and fair, too. Cindy knew in her heart that Grant had surfed as strongly as she had, but the ocean had been kinder to Cindy and sent her the right wave.

Nicole kept squeezing her hand, and Mollie was clapping and shouting. "I knew you could. Didn't I tell you? It always works. Pretending you'll win."

It took a couple of seconds—a couple of long seconds—before the boys started over. But when they did, they ran. Suddenly Cindy felt Duffy lift her high into the air. Everyone was congratulating her at once. And Grant was there. She heard him saying something about her being a great surfer. But then everything got very loud and confusing. And Duffy and Joey and the rest of the guys hoisted her onto their shoulders and paraded her around the bonfire.

When they put her down, Cindy looked around. But Grant was nowhere to be seen.

Chapter 15

*F*lames from the bonfire leapt high into the early-evening sky. Along the western horizon, beyond the oil rigs, yellow and violet stripes of light lingered over the darkening water. Bruce Springsteen's gravelly voice blared from someone's tape deck, almost drowning out the noise of the waves breaking on the shore.

Cindy had never felt happier in her whole life. She was a winner. She was—as Duffy had said when he ran up to her—born to win, and she loved the feeling more than anything in the world. She felt that her heart was leaping higher than the bonfire, but the competition wasn't over for Cindy. She hadn't won what really counted, not yet.

She looked around for Grant. He had to be somewhere. She vaguely remembered him in the press of kids gathered around her after the judges announced the final scores, and she could hear his voice clear as day, "That was great, Cindy. Some of the best surfing I've ever seen." Then he was gone.

Cindy's heart stopped as she looked for Grant among the shadowy figures jostling around the hibachis for burgers and hot dogs. What if Grant had gone home?

Then she spotted him: a tall, muscular guy in sweats, standing on the outskirts of the crowd, a hot dog in his hand. It was too dark and the firelight too flickering to see his face clearly, but she knew it was him. No one else looked quite like that: so strong, so handsome, and— Cindy noticed for the first time—so vulnerable and a little lonely. Cindy took a deep breath and marched toward him, trying to avoid the kids who wanted to stop and talk to her about her performance.

"Grant," she said as she came up behind him.

He turned around, a tentative smile crossing his face. "Yeah?"

"It's my turn now," Cindy said haltingly. "To congratulate you. I didn't get a chance before."

Grant gave a tight little laugh. "Congratulate me?"

Cindy nodded. "You were great today. The way

you rode that curl in.... I've never seen anything like it."

"You should have seen yourself." Grant returned the compliment.

Cindy shrugged, but she was blushing with pleasure in the dark. There was an awkward moment of silence between them. "I guess I came over here to talk," Cindy finally said lamely.

Grant regarded her for a second. His expression was serious. "Yes, we've got a lot to talk about, don't we?" he said, his face slowly lighting up with a smile.

Cindy heaved a sigh of relief. "You'd better believe it. Except, can we get away—from all this?" Cindy gestured toward the crowd. Kids were dancing now. Any division between guys and girls was gone. Couples had already paired off. Nicole was probably sharing her Movable Feasts picnic with Mark. Mollie's short figure was nowhere to be seen. But before Cindy could worry about her sister, her eyes widened as she spotted Anna and Duffy sneaking off toward the parking lot, holding hands.

"How about over by the marina?" Grant suggested. "The dock's a nice place to sit and talk."

Five minutes later they sat side by side, legs dangling over the pier. The moon had risen over the Mesa rock and was casting a broad silvery path across the water. Cindy broke the silence between them with a contented sigh and glanced sideward at Grant. He was tossing shells he had gathered on the beach into the water. She closed her eyes a second and listened to the splash of shells hitting water, then opened them again. Grant was still there.

She couldn't help but remember the last time she had sat there, after her first "date" with Grant. She was with Winston, crying her eyes out, hating the world, and feeling very miserable and alone. Maybe it was part of being fifteen years old, but forty-eight hours later the whole picture had changed. Cindy had a feeling she'd never really get used to these changes, but this was one change she decided she definitely liked.

Still there was the business of talking to Grant. "Grant—" she started.

"No," he interrupted. "Let me talk first, please." He bit his lip, then looked her directly in the eye. He smiled shyly and began. "I wasn't kidding—or being polite—back there. You really are the best I've ever seen. And I knew that last Saturday down on the beach, and I got upset."

"But so did I!" Cindy interrupted.

Grant lifted his hand. "Please, let me finish." Suddenly Cindy realized that whatever Grant had to say, it was hard for him to say it. Instinctively her hand reached across the narrow space between them. Knowing that he sometimes had a hard time expressing himself made her feel better. She rested her fingers lightly on his arm. He looked at her quickly but didn't move his arm away. He talked softly, a real urgency in his voice. "I didn't get upset because you were good—not really. I liked that. I felt—I feel—we have a lot in common. But I guess I thought you only went out there to show me up. To prove something—no—to prove you were better than me. And I freaked out—I guess," he stammered.

"Oh, Grant!" Cindy cried. "I'm sorry. Because ..." Cindy took her hand away from his arm, inhaled sharply, and held on to the edge of the pier very hard. She began talking very fast, almost running the words together. "You're right. I did feel that way. I thought I never saw anyone surf better than you, and I got angry and jealous and figured that you just wanted to show us California kids—to show *me*—up."

Grant gulped. "You felt that? But I never wanted to do that, Cindy. Never. I just wanted to fit in."

Again Cindy reached for his arm. But her hand landed on his hand, and he closed his fingers around hers. For a second Cindy totally forgot whatever it was she had started to say. But she willed her mind clear. "It doesn't matter now, does it? I mean, we both proved we were good. I just lucked out on a better wave."

"I'm beginning to think we both lucked out." Grant's voice was soft and full of feeling. "I guess I just wanted you to notice me, Cindy. To like me ..." His voice trailed off. "At first I thought you might be Duffy's girl."

"To notice you?" Cindy was incredulous. "Me and Duffy?" She started giggling at the thought. Then she remembered that Grant was new in town. She sensed Grant's body tighten up. "But Grant, couldn't you tell? I did like you!" Cindy blurted out. "Oh, I mean I do!" Suddenly her face went all red. She was glad Grant didn't have X-ray eyes or anything and couldn't see her very clearly in the dark.

Then Grant squeezed her hand. He kept staring straight ahead as he admitted in a small voice, "I guess I didn't realize that. I don't have much experience in the girl department."

Cindy's eyes widened, and then her expression softened. He was only sixteen, a year older than she. Why should a sixteen-year-old guy be so very different from a fifteen-year-old girl? She laughed softly. "Me, too. I mean, I've never held a guy's hand before."

And then Grant turned toward her. Even in the moonlight she could see the surprised look on his face. Impulsively, Cindy leaned over and kissed him very quickly on the cheek. A silly lopsided smile crossed his face.

She pulled back, suddenly scared that she had done something wrong. "I'm sorry," she started to apologize, and began scrambling to her feet. But Grant's arm was around her, and he kissed her. This time they kissed on the lips.

"Winston, no!" a voice warned from the far end of the pier.

Cindy and Grant instantly sprang apart and scrambled to their feet. "Mollie, what are you doing here?" Cindy roared, her face turning bright red.

Winston bounded happily past Cindy toward Grant's side. Mollie, emerging from the shadows, giggled nervously. "Uh—I followed you— I brought you some quiches, you know, from Nicole's picnic." She talked very fast and backed slowly away from Cindy.

"When I get a hold of you!" Cindy threatened, and started toward her sister.

"Oooh!" Mollie screeched, and half tumbled off the edge of the pier onto the sand. She bolted down the beach.

Cindy and Grant eyed each other for only a second. A conspiratorial smile passed between them.

"The fourteen-year-old?" Grant asked.

"The fourteen-year-old," Cindy stated.

Instantly the couple sprang off the pier and onto the dark sand. Mollie was running down the beach, her short legs pumping furiously. But Mollie was no athlete, and within seconds Cindy and Grant were alongside her.

Grant grabbed one arm, Cindy the other. Mollie was screaming at the top of her lungs, but from the crazy smile on her face, Cindy knew that her kid sister was enjoying every minute of being chased by the Incredible Hunk.

"Shall we?" Grant asked.

"You bet!" Cindy answered, but as they picked up the giggling, squirming Mollie and stomped out into the water, swinging her over the waves, Cindy yelled above the noise of the surf, "But watch out, Grant. Mollie's the Lewis who just loves being rescued."

Here's a look at what's in store for you in THE KISS, book three in the "Sisters" series for GIRLS ONLY.

The pounding was the first thing Mollie Lewis heard when she woke up that Monday morning. Thump-thump, thump-thump. It sounded like a giant sledgehammer, but it was actually her heart—beating hard enough to wake her up from a sound sleep. At first she thought it had something to do with the dream she'd just had. Then she remembered. Today was T-Day—Theater Day—the day she'd find out if she'd won a part in Vista High's fall musical production.

Unlike Cindy, Mollie was no athlete. But she felt she must have set a new speed record, dashing from the bicycle racks outside the stately, Spanish-style school building through the crowded halls to the auditorium. But there was nothing on the bulletin board next to the double-doored entryway except a hand-lettered sign that said "Beat West Side"—a reference to that weekend's football game against Vista's major rival.

Twice during the morning Mollie dashed back to the auditorium between classes. But there was still no list posted. The tension of not knowing was beginning to make her head ache, and even though she tried to keep her mind on school and off theater, it was difficult. Luckily, no one seemed to notice—until French I.

Her French teacher, Mrs. Preston, had caught her daydreaming in class and sentenced her to stay after school for a disciplinary lecture.

Dejectedly she walked into the hallway, followed closely by her friends Sarah and Linda.

"Tough luck in there," Linda said.

"Yeah, it easily could have been me," Sarah added. "I was daydreaming about Andrew. I'm seeing him next period."

"Say no more," Linda said. Andrew Wedekind was Sarah's latest crush.

Mollie mumbled a few words of encouragement, but her heart wasn't in it. She was too upset at herself for getting in trouble with Mrs. Preston.

Her run-in with the teacher was still gnawing at her an hour later as she walked into the cafeteria for lunch.

Mollie set her tray across from her friend on the Formica tabletop. "So when's the big date?" she asked.

Sarah's face fell. "What date?" she grumbled, casting a wary look toward the middle of the room, where Andrew was seated.

"You mean he didn't ask you?"

Sarah shook her head glumly.

"There I go, sticking my foot in my mouth again," Mollie said with a sigh. "So why the sugar-coated grin?"

Sarah brightened. "It was for you, Mollie. Congratulations."

Linda, sitting alongside Sarah, leaned over and patted Mollie's arm. "Yeah, way to go," she said. "I knew you had it in you."

Linda was right. The cast list was there, and the first name at the top was Mollie Lewis, with "Sandy" typed a few spaces away. Mollie moved her index finger across the line, making sure that her eyes weren't playing tricks on her. But it was true.

Mollie sank down by the auditorium doors. She was too excited to go back to the cafeteria and needed time to compose herself. In her heart she'd known that—eventually—she'd land a role in a Vista High production. But she'd never figured it would happen so soon, in her freshman year. Realizing she'd beaten out dozens of upperclassmen made her proud—but nervous, too. Would she really be able to pull it off?

Attention—GIRLS ONLY!

Sign up here for your
free subscription to Fawcett's new

GIRLS ONLY NEWSLETTER

(for all girls 18 & under)

You'll get the latest
news on trends, 'behind-the-scenes'
looks at your favorite authors,
a Question and Answer column,
and
much, much more...

For your free subscription,
just fill out the coupon below
and mail to:

FAWCETT BOOKS, GIRLS ONLY
201 East 50th Street
New York, NY 10022

Name_____Age_____

Address_____

City_____State_____Zip_____

TAF-68